Bad Associations Spoil Useful Habits

by
Terry Desjardins

Table of Contents

Part 1- I'm your Backroom Man (Early 2006)

Taze stood near the back of the Kingdom Hall and gazed at the front of the Kingdom Hall. He saw a fat bald elder in an unintentionally tight-fitting suit approach him from about twenty feet away. The fat bald elder, Brother Rusty Choker, lumbered toward him with a determined gait. When he finally reached Taze he put out his hand to shake and with a large smiled bellowed, "Hello, Brother Felix!" His voice projected through the Kingdom Hall as if he greeted a Circuit Assembly audience.

Taze responded timidly, "Hello, Brother Choker."

Brother Choker cut through the small talk and asked, "Can you meet with Brother Simmons and myself in the backroom after the meeting?"

The three brothers sat in the backroom.

"Brother Felix, do you know why we asked you to talk to us?"

Taze couldn't find the exact words for a reply.

"Well, Brother Felix, we noticed that your hair is getting long."

Taze sat and stared.

"We want you to make progress in the congregation and in the organization. We want you to gain Jehovah's favor."

Brother Simmons continued, "Brother Felix, we want you to know that we appreciate it when you drive some of the older ones in the congregation to the

1

weekly meetings. Jehovah will certainly bless you for this. We also appreciate your timely answers at our book study on Tuesday nights."

Brother Simmons paused for a moment and looked at the floor. His triple chin trembled. He inflated his cheeks as he painfully searched for his next words. Then he said, "We really want you to progress. In fact, Sister Simmons and I had an excellent time the other night when you had supper with us at our home. I know you're not accustomed to southern food, but I certainly hope you enjoyed it."

Brother Choker interjected. He had an uneasy look on his face, and said hesitantly, "We feel that maybe before you get up on the stage and address the flock for your next number two talk assignment that you trim your hair a bit. It's a bit on the long side, and you know that we have to set a proper example for the flock."

He paused and leaned forward toward Taze. Only about an inch separated their chins. Then, in almost a whisper, he said to Taze, "I'm starting to think that maybe the world has had a negative effect on your attitude. Maybe that education of yours and all that worldly philosophy has influenced you."

Taze lost focus. He was almost thirty, and he could feel his will to live slipping away.

"Brother Felix, we think that maybe you should consider a haircut. Now don't get us wrong. We love your hair. In fact, if the society would let me, I'd grow it long myself," said Brother Simmons. Then he looked over at Brother Chocker and asked, "Don't you agree Rusty?"
"I agree Dale, but I don't have to worry about hair anymore." The two elders shared a chuckle over Brother Choker's fat bald head. Taze only stared.

After reading a scripture and sharing a prayer, the backroom meeting ended.

Taze agreed to cut his hair.

"Thanks for staying after, Brother Felix."
"You're welcome, Brother Choker. Thank you, Brother Simmons." Taze managed to smile as he walked away.

Taze went home and listened to two messages on his answering machine:

1. Taze, are you at the meeting? Your uncle had to go to the hospital today.
2. Hey Taze, this is Akari. I'm so sorry, but I can't make it tonight. I have some stuff I really need to do. Bye.

The two messages did not improve his mood.

Taze only had two associates. Horace Brewer, a Jehovah's Witness business owner and Denny Wister, a worldly hermit lawyer that roomed with Horace. Both grew up with Taze in the post-industrial wasteland of Cleveland, Ohio.

Then there was Akari Zak, a worldly poetry professor of Japanese descent. Taze taught at the same university and met her two months earlier at a faculty meeting.

Taze thought of the disappointment of the two messages. He thought, "Damn, my aunt calls to tell me about my uncle in the hospital again, and Akari breaks a date. Stuff to do! What does that mean? What stuff? I'm the one who has to go to five meetings a week. And my uncle again! Maybe if he would stop drinking so much."

He sat on his couch and looked at the ceiling fan vibrate. Five months earlier, he relocated to Richmond, Virginia to teach literature.

He thought back to a childhood memory of his aunt, who raised him in The Watchtower.

He could not date as a teenager. One time a worldly girl called him, but his aunt didn't approve of any sort of social interaction with a member of the opposite sex until he was past the bloom of youth.

The worldly girl waited on the phone for Taze to speak, but Taze stayed silent because his aunt listened in. He waited patiently for his aunt to hang up. She didn't. Finally, Taze said hello. The worldly girl responded.

After a moment, his aunt spoke, "I'm sorry, but Taze is not old enough to date because he is not old enough to get married."

With the perils of dating as a young Jehovah's Witness, Taze found it incredibly difficult to confidently navigate communication with Akari.

Akari was only twenty-five years old. She was already an exceptional scholar who produced brilliant publications. Unlike Taze, she was from a privileged background.

Taze, lost in thought, said to himself, "Who cares about her? She's just another illusion."

The phone rang again, and he answered. He knew it was his aunt. His aunt always worried, always imagined the worst-case scenarios for every human event because the end of this system of things was so close. She'd always remind him that "Bad associations spoil useful habits!"

4

"Hello."

"What are you doing?"

"Nothing. Just eating some soup. What are you doing?"

"Your uncle had surgery today."

"Really."

"Your cousin is going through hell. She won't let him visit here on his vacation."

Taze didn't want to hear the same negative stuff about his uncle or his cousin's lousy Jehovah's Witness marriage again.

"I have to go," mumbled Taze.

He hung up the phone. He had to work the next day. His job irritated him. He lectured to disinterested students who took his required entry-level literature course. He overcame all of the discouragement that The Watchtower presented about higher education, and actually finished his Ph.D. Yet, he continued to feel overwhelming despair even after he began to separate himself from the organization.

As a young child, his uncle developed a serious drinking problem while serving as an elder in the local congregation of Jehovah's Witnesses. Taze kept his uncle's alcoholism a secret.

The Watchtower existed as the central part of his life. He attended meetings every Sunday, Monday, and Friday. His family, through the instructions of The Governing Body, required unimaginable devotion to the organization. Expulsion and shunning served as consequences for sex before marriage, saying negative things about the "organization," smoking weed, and a giant list of other things. Expulsion, or as it's called, disfellowshipping, produced fear in every Jehovah's Witness. It meant being unable to talk to close family members or any other member of the congregation.

That is why so many years later, Taze still attended meetings.

*   *   *

Text message: I fart.

A simple message from Horace Brewer. Horace always talked about cleansing his bowel. Horace texted poems.

Faith healers were consulted
ministers and medicine men
herbalists.
Priests and seers
Elders and Nay Sayers

The bowel: Horace concerned himself with it for at least twenty percent of an average day. He lived with Denny. Denny sat in a small dusty computer room (8 hard drives) and typed and programmed and surfed the web. He'd check on Denny to see if he completed the work for the day. Denny spent evenings preparing a will and a divorce a month where he pocketed maybe $1000. His diet consisted of easily prepared foods or whatever involved no preparation at all, like microwavable oatmeal, bananas, figs, handfuls of cereal, and toasted frosted wheat.

Horace rarely admitted fault for anything at all, particularly with his business. "Why do these people keep calling me?" Denny would calmly explain to Horace that "when you own a business, people will call. Especially people that give you money." Taze moved to northern Virginia to associate with these two guys.

Taze thought of Akari, the Japanese hipster two buildings over. She wore baggy aids quilt skirts tied at the waist by shoelaces and sometimes she let her hair bangs grow over her eyes. Her long earrings always dangled, and she bragged about her jewelry design.

She'd always start with a big smile that excited Taze, but within a minute, her conversation always gravitated to her boyfriend, her family, her indie rock, or her imagination. As a poetry professor, she created some of the finest visions imaginable, and when Taze read her published book, he fell in love with the "she" that always seemed to be the main character in her writing. One replayed in his head continuously:

She wilts under the warm breath of his tenderness
Mountains surrounding this moment.
As an embrace means forgiveness and cold-water
sprays
From windy snows and ice kisses
She remembered this moment as it passed
Into many forgotten moments of lovers.
In the world of snow angel destiny and
Clouds seeping saliva

Taze felt strange because he had given up belief in ambiguous concepts like the soul, spirits, and Elizabethan romance. He felt uncomfortable waiting for her damn phone calls. Taze tried to embrace a new form of poetry that expressed love instead of overt disgust and desolation. The phone rang:

Horace- Hi, Taze
Taze- Hi, how's your bowel today?

Although this would normally be an unusual question to ask, it came perfectly natural for Taze to ask Horace that question.

Horace- Let me read you what I wrote to my herbalist:
The program is going pretty well.
I'm on my second week and feel good.
I will probably end up doing it a second time.
The bowel is still not regular and hasn't been for three years.

I really need to get this corrected and would like to talk to you about focusing on just that for a couple of weeks.

The regulator is causing great discomfort in the anus area, and I had to take prep-h to calm that down.

The intestinal sweep hasn't done anything. Also, I still have frequent flare ups in my upper abdomen.

Side note:

I've included a hair-loss site with two very good products:

Thymuskin (I really think you will dig the concept of thinning hair being an auto-immune response).

And Rivivogen.

See what you can come up with. Perhaps we can work on this one together.

I really like your program. It's very no nonsense. Also, that nerve stuff is amazing, and the anxiety formula is working great now.

Horace- Was that okay? What I wrote?

Taze- Yes, it's fine.

*   *   *

Taze woke up, and he ran through the shower. When he looked into the foggy morning mirror, his confidence yielded a little, and he solemnly shaved his sideburns.

He walked into class. Some students sipped coffee, while others slept. Some read giant textbooks. A thought popped up in Taze's mind. "Maybe I should have them read a paragraph from my book?" Taze pulled it up on his laptop and projected it on the screen. Okay, folks, let's read this paragraph together:

The moon shone brightly overhead as the young man approached the doorknob trembling with fright. His aunt warned him about this moment many years before. He imagined the father, tall, well-groomed, and smart. He imagined the mother in a long designer dress. His nerves overwhelmed him. Although the young woman liked him, he felt wildly uncomfortable in meeting her parents. He pictured a fireplace and a mantel with dozens of pictures and dogs barking in the background. He saw academic awards from older siblings and complex books laying gently on waxed tables.

So, class, what is your impression of this first paragraph? Student number 127 stood up in the vague distance and yelled, "It's really sappy." Several students laughed.

After class he visited Akari's room and peaked in. She, coincidentally enough, shared her poetry with her class. "So, class, what do you think?" she asked.

One student responded, "Brilliant. It relays the raw existential beauty of pure being, during those all too rare moments of requited love." She blushed with modesty, and Taze walked away from the room and threw his hair pick against the wall and broke the middle prong. He wondered if his students knew who wrote the paragraph he shared when another student stated, "This must have been written by a love-struck middle schooler."

"Shit. I can't believe who I am. Goddamn." Taze's phone rang. His aunt.
Aunt- Taze, your uncle just got out of the hospital.
Taze- Really? That's nice. I'm sorry. I have a class coming in. I have to go.
Aunt- Go to the meeting tomorrow! Don't miss it.

The endless stream of desperate thoughts kept entertaining themselves in Taze's mind. He felt disgraced and discouraged.

"Professor Felix," said Akari.

"Hi, Dr. Zak. Your class is great. You do an excellent job."

"Thank you. Did you get my message? I'm sorry for canceling."

She walked away briskly while the insides of Taze liquified with nerves.

Taze entered his second class of the day and decided to share the first paragraph of his novel with the class. He thought that "maybe the first class just didn't get it."

"Welcome," Taze faked a pleasant mood, "Welcome class, have a seat, get comfortable." He projected the paragraph again. Okay, let's read this together:

The moon shone brightly overhead as the young man approached the doorknob trembling with fright. His aunt warned him about this moment many years before. He imagined her father, tall, well-groomed, and smart. He imagined the mother in a long designer dress. His nerves overwhelmed him. Although the young woman liked him, he felt wildly uncomfortable in meeting her parents. He pictured a fireplace and a mantel with dozens of pictures and dogs barking in the background. He saw academic awards from older siblings and complex books laying gently on waxed tables.

"Any first impressions?" Taze meekly asked his class. A student wearing a "Hands off Iraq" tee shirt raised his hand, "I have a comment." Taze listened with anticipation. "It seems to me that a nervous unselfconfident man wrote this. It's almost as if he's scared to do anything. I get the sense that the writer is painting a picture of a really scared dude. Like this guy listens to 1970s soft rock and cries to himself in the shower."

"Thank you. Your name?"

"Z"

"Thank you, Z. Any other questions or comments?"

Another student raised her hand. She had several tattoos on her arms and nose rings. "Professor Felix, Do you feel that maybe the introduction is a prelude of some sort of confession of impotence or sterility?"

"Okay, thank you. Let's move on, I believe we were reading um . . . um . . . yes, chapter three of *Tender is the Night* by F. Scott Fitzgerald.

*   *   *

"Taze Felix," said the receptionist at the doctor's office. "Taze Felix," she repeated in a louder voice. "Mr. Felix? Dr. Turgev is ready for you."

Taze walked down the hallway to the backroom and sat down.

"So, Mr. Felix. What do you do for a living?"
"I am an adjunct professor of Literature, and I write academic articles and books."
"Where do you live?"
"Richmond."
"Via where? You don't seem like a local."
"Cleveland, Ohio."
"Oh, the mistake by the lake."
"Yes. That's it."
"Describe your childhood."
"Desperation . . ."
"Um . . . let's just keep it literal, no elaborate metaphors or poetic treatises, please."
"Born in Cleveland and raised by my aunt and uncle as a Jehovah's Witness."
"I see. What happened to your biological parents?"
"Well, my mother got hooked on drugs, and my father is missing. He left one day and never returned."
"Okay. So, your aunt and uncle raised you as Jehovah's Witness?"
"Yes. It seems they were searching for something amidst the rhythm of the sixties and found a religious

11

cult and joined with their whole hearts. I am the result of that decision."

"Okay. Was it an oppressive cult?"

"I think so."

"Describe it a little."

"We had these things called congregation picnics in which enormous Polish women ate giant mountainous sausages and filled their eyes with sauerkraut visions. They added barbeque sauce to the tiny wieners and once a mechanic brought an acoustic guitar and played a bald-headed version of 'Earth Angel.' Sometimes the macaroni and cheese was homemade and sometimes it came from a box. Generally, the Garlengars were the life of the event with their pinochle cards, and there was a specific time when Emory and Keefe played chess to a desperately boring stalemate."

"Okay. It seems that you have a tough time being literal. You escape your trauma via your imagination. Keep going."

"Um . . . the garage was like an ancient pyramid tomb with what seemed like tunnels and pathways that may have led to some kind of divine entry way. Regardless, the picnic tables were foldable and plastic with plastic taped to them at the corners. Maybe one of the Beagley's might arrive ten or twelve minutes early and tape the corners up to avoid the cleaning of the messy Fleese kids' spills. All of the chairs said property of some Watchtower congregation on the bottom, actually not all of them. Two wooden chairs in particular had Schictel carved or perhaps engraved into the oak."

As he told the doctor these memories, he wondered about the day of the carving. A switchblade maybe and the fat blood splotched, old, marked hands of the entrepreneur claiming the chairs as his and only his, and Taze thought of how he felt guilty for sitting in one of those chairs.

He continued, "One time it rained, and we all had to enter the house. I recall a chandelier, so glittery and sparkly that it felt like Jehovah was there. He must have been in this house somewhere. The television dominated the landscape of the living room with a super-sized church organ that played rhythms contrary to the mood of the event. The surprise I felt in my heart in 1984 when he displayed a strange looking piece of technology called a computer."

"Who was this guy?"

"Schictel."

"Why does he matter to these memories?"

"He was just another big part of early life. A life of demonstrable sadness. Of demands unearthly for such a young child, a belief system. Ah . . . um. . . a . . . I don't know . . . ah . . . I was presented with an array of various mostly overweight old people. I sat in station wagons on Saturday mornings."

*   *   *

Akari had to take some sort of entrance exam related to a post-doctoral program. Taze once had motivation and ambitiously sought more education. She was still motivated and sunshiny happy with her solid family structure and omnibenevolent poetry. So, in turn, she took an entrance exam for a difficult program. In fact, Akari seemed nervous about the exam, so in order to lighten up the situation Taze sent her a text message quote from one of her favorite novels, *The Confederacy of Dunces*:

"Good Luck with the exam. But who knows how the sometimes-ruinous wheel of Fortuna will turn!"

She replied angrily: "I don't understand. Is that a good luck wish? Or a good luck, but I think you are going to do bad statement?"

*   *   *

Back at the Kingdom Hall:

"Brother Felix, we noticed you're only pretending to sing the Kingdom Melodies. Brother Leaflet was sitting directly behind you and couldn't hear a word you were supposed to be singing. Now some of us don't have the greatest voices in the world, but you have to understand that we must sing praises to Jehovah. By the way Brother, some of the older ones in the congregation find your perfume or cologne, what do they call that for men? Anyway, they find your scent maybe a tad or a bit overpowering. Personally, I find your scent perfectly fine, but you know, for the sake of some of the older ones in the congregation, could you abstain from it?"

"No problem, Brother Choker."

"Oh, and don't forget about that haircut."

He got back to his house, and Horace waited on the toilet with the door wide opened while he read a copy of *The Brothers Karamazov*.

"Hey Taze! I made a salad. It's in the fridge."

Taze looked in the fridge to notice a large white plastic bowl with garbanzo beans, alfalfa, feta cheese, and a gooey green substance. "What's the green stuff?"

Horace had taken his shirt off by then. "It's liquid chlorophyll. It cleanses your colon, supposedly. I think it's working. Look at how green this toilet tissue is." Horace smiled and proudly held the tissue in the air for Taze to examine. "It sure is green." He walked back into the kitchen and blended the leftover garbanzo beans with some olive oil and garlic. He dipped some lime tortilla chips. He ate his dinner as he opened up a can of ice beer. He drank and drank for the numbness and to, hopefully, forget the text message disaster with Akari.

Horace gave it one last wipe and produced a fart that reverberated off the walls in the living room. The

14

couch cushion vibrated from the toilet flush as Taze watched Horace gallop toward him while he swallowed an organic beet juice Xanax cocktail. Horace left muddy footprints on the carpet.

"How was the meeting?"

"They talked to me about the singing. I just can't bring myself to sing those depressing songs anymore. Number 27, 'From House to House,' is particularly depressing."

"Yes, I know. I'm sure that song has clogged my colon once or twice. I haven't enjoy the singing since the purple songbook."

"It clogs my brain. It seems like I can't think or function at any human level mentally during that music." In the melody of 'From House to House' Taze hummed, "Bah Bah, Bah Bah, Bah Bah, Bah Bah, Bah, Bah, Bah Bah, Bah Bah."

Horace smiled and responded, "The kingdom melodies haunt my dreams. Want some beet juice?"

"No, but I'll take the Xanax. Actually, I was at the doctor and told him about the congregation picnics."

"What did the doctor say?"

"He said that I use my imagination to escape the trauma."

*   *   *

Another dinner invitation led Taze to the house of a congregation elder and his family. Taze felt overly despondent and couldn't bear to join the frivolity of the conversation about deteriorating world conditions and the nearness of Armageddon.

Taze really had to prepare psychologically for this situation, a context where he felt like screaming into the air. Everyone was nice enough. The house was well decorated with thousands of wallpaper flowered designs. Definitely not modern. The elder's wife invited a sister to meet Taze.

15

"Taze. This is Sister Becky Ebberson."
"Becky. This is Brother Taze Felix."
"Nice to meet you, Becky."
"Nice to meet you too, Taze."
"So, where are you from?"
"I'm from here in Virginia."

"Oh lord," Taze thought, "even worse than a Witness girl, a Witness girl from these parts." Taze said, "Oh wow, that's cool. I really like the area."
"Where are you from?" she asked.

Taze wanted to give this witness girl a complete answer, one where she would realize everything, particularly his mental issues. He wanted to say, "Well, Becky, this cult has messed up my head and combined with the Cleveland, Ohio steel plant exodus depression, government housing, mass poverty and hunger, aesthetic disasters, frozen lakes and freezing snow, and an alcoholic elder uncle, I cannot have a normal relationship with anybody or anything."

Instead, he answer meekly, "Cleveland, Ohio."
The fat elder piped in, "Taze is a professor of . . . what subject?"
"Literature. An adjunct professor."

The obese hand gestured as he spoke and put more canned salsa on his plate, "He's a smart one, a real intellectual. We just have to get him to raise his hand more at the meetings." Taze felt impotent. Brothers who answered at meetings "turned on" most sisters. Every meeting repeated the same material. The answers always directly corresponded to material in a paragraph. For example, the paragraph might state that "God is love" and its corresponding question might ask, "What is God?" Taze felt uncomfortable raising his hand and answering. He preferred depth, research, study, and long explanatory answers that

16

required critical thinking. The Watchtower didn't offer that.

"So, Taze," asked Becky, "What do you like to read?" Taze couldn't be honest. He wanted to say, "Henry Miller, D.H. Lawrence, Jean Paul Sartre, Friedreich Nietzsche, and Karl Marx! I read sexually explicit pagan hedonistic poetry of demonic origins and anti-Christ overtures. I read shit that elevates humanity while it simultaneously destroys all moral and social standards of spiritual life. I want the world to become chaos and destruction. I want bridges to collapse. I want the paneling in the basement to peel off spontaneously. I want teeth to decay instantly. I want people to give up and resoundingly renounce all that is sacred to happiness. Joy is unattainable, and freedom is nonsense. Workers of the World Unite!"

He answered calmly, "Well, I really enjoy reading mystery novels, like Agatha Christie. What do you like to do for fun?"
"Movies, getting together with the friends, like this. I like to study the bible and go out in service."
The obese elder interrupted, "Becky is a regular pioneer."
Taze managed a smile and looked forward blankly.

The conversation at the dinner party seemed endless. It's not that Taze disliked people or company or fellowship, it's that he had to literally think of how to behave in these particular social contexts. He had to ask himself: what are the social precedents for this context? What do I say when someone asks, "How are you?" How do I respond when someone requests the beans to be passed? These were hard questions for Taze. It was much easier for him to answer questions about *Simulacra and Simulation* or to explain Transcendentalism.

17

The dinner moved naturally to the living room where they played games of chance with dice, pieces, and little knobs of plastic that moved around colorful boards. Interestingly enough, the elder pulled out a game called "Your Life." In that life, Taze became a doctor, a father of three, and he took vacations to Belize. He seemed very stable. His little plastic car moved around the board and effortlessly landed on money, family, wealth, prestige, honor, religion, and, finally, he finished in first place. He was able to leave his family oodles of money and land.

When he arrived home, he was welcomed with a virtual orgy of organic remedies. Horace covered every little space on the kitchen counters and tables with cures and colon cleansers. Dark green liquids, wheaty grains, B vitamins, gabad, humus chickpeas, various garlics that emitted odors opening pores in noses, liver beets, giant mushrooms shaped like t-bone steaks, stringy salad greens that resembled magnified sperm, powders and valerian, snortable melatonin, injectable 5-htp, every possible natural product for anxiety relief or colonic matter dispensing.

Horace laid face down on the sofa, clearly upset.
"Horace? Horace? What's wrong?"
"I'm having those same old thoughts again. You know the thoughts of like . . . um . . . well . . . like emptiness and meaninglessness."
"Remember Jeff?" asked Horace.
Taze didn't respond.
"He got disfellowshipped."
"Ah man, that sucks. I remember him. He was cool. What did he do?"
"What do you think! He had sex."

Horace started to moan.

Taze scratched his head and asked, "Do you want to get some junk food and watch our favorite movie, *Ulee's Gold*?"

"Maybe later. Just let me be for now."

Taze walked upstairs to his room and checked his email. He was excited for one second when he saw an email from Akari, but it turned out to be a forwarded picture of cats. He heard a moan from downstairs. Horace was really getting deep inside himself. The misery filled the house like carbon monoxide, but tonight, it would not be fatal.

*   *   *

The next day Taze ran into Akari at work. "Did you see how beautiful the moon was this morning?" she asked.

At first Taze wanted to lie and tell her how he did notice its beauty and that he felt that they looked up at it at the same exact moment and how he wrote the poem:

Moon's dawn looks down upon beauty looking up.

Another answer that came to his mind was more like, "Who cares about that celestial body that only reminds us that we are infinitely small and alone and without purpose." Taze went with the standard, "Yes, I did. It was really bright."

Akari walked away with her brightness, and Taze stood alone and looked at the stained cement ground under his feet.

Taze entered his class. "Okay folks, let's read the second paragraph from that novel we started."

The moon shone brightly overhead as the young man approached the doorknob trembling with fright. His aunt warned him about this moment many years before. He imagined the father, tall, well-groomed, and smart. He imagined the mother in a long designer dress. His nerves overwhelmed him. Although the young woman liked him, he felt wildly uncomfortable in meeting her parents. He pictured a fireplace and a mantel with dozens of pictures and dogs barking in the background. He saw academic awards from older siblings and complex books laying gently on waxed tables.

"That's the first paragraph," a student yelled.
"You're right. You remembered!"
"Of course, I remembered. Who could forget!"
Students laughed.
"Okay. Let's give the second paragraph a chance."

He could not explain the jittery trembling of his nerve endings. They seemed to be contracting simultaneously, which led to uncontrollable vibrations. Suddenly the door opened, and a very beautiful and elegant woman answered. She was in her forties or fifties and stood with straight salt and pepper hair and said, "Come in, Jerome. We've heard so much about you." She turned away and looked upstairs and yelled, "Sandra? Jerome is here to pick you up." Jerome ate two or three almonds from a crystal dish that rested upon a glass table. The father entered. Jerome almost fell getting up, losing his balance. The flowers on the sofa cushion would not have stopped his fall.

The student criticism started quickly. "It's like a scene from a soap opera or something. Like a Hallmark movie my grandma would watch." Then a cell phone started to play a hip-hop song.

This led Taze into a tirade. "You students have no idea of the horrors that you will face or the destructiveness of life. You think life is full of pleasantries and happy surprises? Well, it's not. It's nothing but desolation and sadness. The world is decaying rapidly. You students will drown. You will suffocate. You will cry for your mommies and daddies

20

and grandmothers and aunts and sisters. And guess what? They'll be dead, like everybody else that has ever lived, dead, dead, completely unconscious. They're not angels or prophets or ghosts. They cannot be reached through mediums. They are conscious of nothing. They are dead and nothing will bring them back."

Taze collapsed into his chair. Struck with inquisitive shock, the students slowly dismissed themselves, one at a time.

"What's that dude's problem?"
"What got into him?"
"He's nuts."

The phone rang, and Taze saw that it was his aunt. "Why does she have to call me now!"

"Hello."
"What are you doing?"
"Nothing. Just resting."
"Your cousin is in a mess with that wife. When you get married, please marry a sister that understands submission to her husband."
"Okay. No problem. So, what's up?"
"Your uncle had another one his episodes. We had to rush him into the emergency room."
"That sucks," Taze spoke without much emotion.
"Your cousin is beeping in."
"Okay. Bye"

Horace went back to his own house, so Taze was all alone. He opened up several beers and drank. He took out some paper and attempted some poetry.

I am blinded with contempt for existence.
I am choked with boiling steam that burns my lungs.
I am angered by the desperate struggle for . . .

21

He started another one.

My back is shale covered in lime.
It's growing fungus, and now is mold.
Slowly it is creeping up my neck.
To my brain

He next thought of the comment Akari made that praised the beauty of the moon. Then, his thoughts brought him back to the greasy spoon family restaurant called Mama's Place. It featured a 69-cent breakfast. Two greasy eggs, two slices of greasy stale toast with a pat of dried butter, cup of cold urine coffee, and home fries. Yet all the JWs would eat there after the meeting, due to poverty and hunger. They'd congregate at this smoky classless diner to indulge in food that would certainly clog any organ or intestine until it held the same consistency as the inside of a one-hundred-year-old tree. Each breakfast grew a new ring of caked oil in the lower small intestine. The colon would whimper with saddened spurts of gaseous noise.

He imagined the poetry of the colon. Horace penned this masterpiece of organ art:

Do not treat me to trans-fat to fulfill your fantasy of salty toasted fast-food bun.
Do not present me with the white paste residue of potato sticks.
Please show me angelic olives and field greens with vinegar splattering.
Wheat germ is my sexual indulgence.
I laid with oatmeal in several prune juice baths.
I climbed the fig tree naked and enjoyed the scrape of orgasmic passion against the fibrous bark with joyous splinters.

Taze remembered his uncle whom everyone seemed to love, especially those in the congregation. They looked up to him with admiration as he gave long scripted bible talks. People looked at these talks with the respect early 15th century popes enjoyed. But for Taze, he lived in desperation in a repressed household of fictional mythology that ruled the belief and social structure of the "family." His uncle made everybody feel good, no matter how poor or mentally unstable. That seemed to be his uncle's job as an elder in the congregation. Clearly stated, he helped mentally ill and extraordinarily depressed people feel good about themselves. He helped people that lacked friends or faced emotional difficulties with ordinary things like waking up. He made them feel special. The Watchtower taught everlasting life, and his uncle made people feel like they wanted to live forever and that he'd be the guy they'd live forever with. But for all of the grandeur, his uncle could not stop drinking.

Akari provided a whole other element of sadness. Her worldly ways, an untouchable woman from the perspective of The Watchtower that always advised against becoming unevenly yoked. Taze lamented, "Akari . . . the way random shirts and trendy sweaters lay messy in your car, and how I imagine your house crumbling with disorganization and empty hummus containers and burned-out rolling papers with glass pipe with black brick fireplace unused for years and orange painted blank walls and papers and papers of unpublished and forgotten revised poetry that speaks to the saints of the contemporary wine bar scene. And sometimes I see you and think of how plain you are with no lipstick or maybe such a light shade that it's only noticeable to you. Why do you carry a perfect combination of class and 'slumming it' poverty?"

Take off my tie.
Slide if off after the knot is unfurled
Free my neck.
With your fingernail whims
Let the redness of your sultry touch
rub its prints into my bubbling shivers.

23

Make invisible hairs stand.
Nurture their fragility with softness
One by one.
Hesitate, teasing momentary buzz intoxication
We harmonize breathes heavily
and fall.

We fall
dizziness from caresses.
Hair follicles folding furiously
Intensity thinks you intensely
Moonlight enters physical equation
And so does slight sweat.

"This can never be," said Taze. "This will never be."

The phone rang, and the caller ID read "unknown caller." Always the scariest of circumstances. Taze did not want to talk to his aunt or cousin or Horace or Denny and probably not even Akari. He went to sleep.

His department chair left a note in Taze's mailbox. It read, "Please see me."

"Hi, Dr. Almand."
"Dr. Felix. Sit down. Let's talk, please."
"Okay, um."
"Let me ask you a few things. Well, rather, I received some official written complaints concerning some comments you made during your class yesterday."
"Yeah, doctor. I can explain, you see . . ."
"No, no, no, I'll ask the questions. It appears according to one student, who wishes to remain anonymous for the time being, that you said, 'Your life is nothing, but desolation and sadness' and another student quoted you as saying, 'You students will drown. You will suffocate. You will cry for your mommies and daddies and grandmothers and aunts and sisters. And guess what? They'll be dead, like everybody else that has ever lived, dead, dead,

completely unconscious.' Can I ask you how this relates to 20th century American Literature?"

"Well, doctor. I . . . um . . . I've been a little stressed lately. I . . . ah . . . um . . . I haven't been myself."

The department head cut him off, "Don't go into details. I understand. Tell you what. Take some time off. Get your life together. We'll give you a leave of absence and when you're ready and healthy enough to return, give us a call. Of course, you know, we can't pay you, but as soon as you're healthy, consider your job here. Okay."

"Um . . . but sir I need to work. I need to . . ."

"Listen, Dr. Felix. We've cut you a lot of slack in this institution. We know that you have, let's say, nihilist tendencies. That doesn't fit in with what this institution is all about. Now take the leave of absence and come back in a year healthy, or you'll be officially let go. Understand?"

"Yes, Dr. Almand."

Taze, obviously dejected, walked by Akari's class to see eager students flailing their hands in the air, and shaking their heads up and down in agreement.

*   *   *

Doctor's appointment:

"Mr. Felix? Mr. Felix? Taze Felix? The doctor is ready to see you."

"That's Dr. Felix."

"What?"

"Never mind."

Taze walked down the long hallway, all the way to the backroom and sat down. The doctor appeared. Taze started to get dizzy and lightheaded.

"So, Mr. Felix, where were we the last time we talked? Oh, I see. Somewhere around 12 years old, I believe. Okay, continue."

"Well, doctor, I just lost my job and . . ."

"Mr. Felix, you weren't working at 12. Stick to your childhood. Just trust me on this."

Taze began to speak, "The stench, the smell, I remember the smell. It was like stale rolled oats combined with petroleum byproducts combined with sweaty mold. It pervaded the entire Cleveland region. It stretched to the suburbs and showed up at high school dances. It launched its own publicity campaign for mayor and almost won. There was this feeling like we were that lost group of people that died in Death Valley. We kept working and surviving, but we were stuck in some desert horror. Some scandalously barren factories with dark clouds as their ceilings and freezing rain as their asbestos. Jobless and hopeless, even inanimate objects breathed horror while humans rusted clean through. Trees choked while railroad ties belched garlic from local perogies. I was only twelve, and I recall a morning on Grape Street when I was about to smoke marijuana with friends immediately after knocking on doors to convert people to The Watchtower. They all drove red Chevettes. The professional football team was a perfect representation of the city. Suddenly people joined religious cults all across the city and walked barefoot with hardened feet to that giant Father Quaker church at the same corner as fat caked restaurants, comic bookstores, a rusted greenhouse with plants that breathed oxygen and gave off carbon dioxide, and a housing district called Agape Canal, where people lived for years and years and ended up mentally deficient because of neon green sprinkler water. I had an uncle who embedded himself to the sofa as a decoration. He watched reruns of *Ozzy and Harriet* and perhaps imagined that his own disastrous childhood was more like Ricky and Dave's. We sang the Ricky songs together, especially the one about having a girlfriend in every country all over the world. He drank beer."

"Okay, Taze. It seems that you sublimate your trauma into your elaborate word play. Have you considered writing a book?"

"Wait, doctor! There's one more thing that I want to say. There was this table that folded out of the wall and on Sunday many of the overweight ones at the congregation would bring slabs of bologna. They spoke occasionally and told us about the garlic of their nether regions, and garlic in their compressed factory intestine lining."

Taze left the doctor's office not feeling much better. He pictured the appointment earlier in the week. He imagined relating the "Disney Girls" Beach Boys lyrics:

Hi, Pop, . . . good morning mom
get up guess what!
I'm in love with a girl I found.
She's really swell
Cause she likes
Church, bingo chances, and old-time dances

And he imagined that the doctor became his uncle and that the office transformed itself into a suburban kitchen table while his two cousins enjoyed food cooked by his aunt. And he imagined the wisdom of advice that flowed from his guardian's mouth like taking life's water free. Advice so valuable, that when swallowed, life became complete and perfect. Taze pictured his family holding hands and hugging at zoos and tumbling on clean full grass. He imagined all of them sharing stories and complimenting each other and treating each other with unconditional love. Taze wanted his doctor to open his mind and make it peaceful, instead, as the appointment ended, he was handed a piece of paper and on it was the name of an antidepressant.

*   *   *

"Brother Felix, how are you tonight? Glad you made it to the meeting. We just need to talk to you for a few minutes in the backroom afterward."

Taze sat motionless during the religious indoctrination session as they asked questions from the platform. Questions Taze heard for twenty-nine years or perhaps since pre-birth. In order to survive these sessions, he concentrated on anything else he could. Unfortunately, his mind slipped and nothing else seemed to help his psyche. So, he tuned in on the information. From the stage, the cocky elder spoke, "Now brothers and sisters, what does it say here in 1 Corinthians 3:23? It says, 'Bad associations spoil useful habits.' What does this mean? It means, do not become unevenly yoked with an unbeliever. Do not associate with those in the Satan's system of things that surrounds you. Do not go to school dances. Do not have workmates as friends. Do not have parties. Do not write poetry. Do not watch R rated movies. Do not . . ." Essentially, it was a list of things Taze could not do. Again, a list that he heard so many times before that he couldn't bear to hear it again. He tuned out of the meeting and tuned into his job loss. That didn't help. So, he tuned out of the job loss and into the awful reality of his relationship with Akari. Then, he tuned out of Akari and into Horace's clogged colon and out of that into his uncle's health problems and then he just went blank and came to in the backroom surrounded by the elders.

"Brother Felix, we noticed that your hair is still a little on the long side. It seems like you still haven't been to the barbershop. I can recommend one if you'd like.   Also, it seems as though one of the sisters drove by your house and heard some loud music coming from your front room. Now, we don't have anything against having parties or what not, but according to the sister, it sounded like the song "That's the Way of the World" by Earth, Wind, and

Fire. Now when I was a young man the only thing we did when we listened to a song like that was fool around with a member of the opposite sex."

"Okay . . . um."

"Let me ask you a question. Do you know that when we do our marriage vows, the elder says to the partners you may now "greet" the bride and not you may now grope the bride and carry on with the bride in front of the audience? Do you know why?"

"Um . . . well. It is immoral to be involved sexually with a woman before marriage."

"Right! Now I'm not saying you had a girl in that house, but the sister swears she saw a silhouette behind the curtains. Can you let us know what happened?"

Taze hadn't been with a woman in a very long time. And he hadn't heard "That's the Way of the World" since he lived in El Paso, Texas several years earlier.

"I really don't know what you're talking about."

"Is your address 1866 Sandra Lane?"

"No. It's 1888 Sandra Lane."

"Okay, well, that's Sister Longfate's mistake then. We'll talk to her later. Why don't you go get yourself a haircut."

Taze stared at himself in the mirror at his pale corpse like frame and whispered, "You're an anti-transcendentalist. Face it. You're an anti-moralist. You're against life. Face it. You're ugly. Face it. Akari deserves sanity. Akari deserves a real artist, somebody that is functional in social groups and can sit and watch music with a glass of wine and converse delicately between songs and sets. She deserves magical natural sunshine park afternoons with blankets of fall leaves colored by God for her. She deserves the popping sound of a cork and the swooshing sound of a natural flowing freshwater spring. She deserves to never be in submission to anyone, especially a man. I am afraid I have been far too corrupted via cult mind control, but I am working on it."

Horace's car pulled into the driveway. "Let's go out man. Let's have some fun."
"I'm not really up for it, Horace. Please, just let me sleep."
"I had a full colon cleanse today and a complete rectal exam. They used a small camera. It was miraculous."
"Okay Horace. One drink."

They entered a small pub and ordered pints of dark beer.

"Man, Taze, the shit that came out of my bowel today looked like this beer. It looked like Lake Erie." They drank another round, and a native Irish band played some traditional songs while very young Irish girls danced kicking their legs upward.

"A lot of it was thick like overdone cheesy mashed potatoes. They filled up these flimsy plastic pouches and I thought, 'damn if that pouch bursts open!' The doctor did notice the wheat germ treatment and the liquid chlorophyll therapy. He said it made the suction a little easier. Damn those bags just filled up, and the stench almost disintegrated my nostrils. So, did you talk to Akari?"
"Not lately. She probably knows that I lost my job. She won't call or nothing."
"Why don't you get over her? Marry a witness. They have to be in subjection to you, and I won't have to shun you like I do Jeff. If you keep pursuing her, and she finally shows an interest, you'll get yourself in trouble. You know what we've learned about the morality of worldly women."
"I know. I know. They're all feminist whores, right?"
"I wouldn't know, but that's what I gather from The Watchtower."

The Irish band packed up and while they drank another round two worldly women approached and said, "Hey guys. Where are your girlfriends?"

Horace spoke up quickly, "Actually, we're single."

"Can we join you?"

Taze tried to speak, but Horace interrupted, "Sure, sit down!"

The two women dressed scantily in short skirts and tight tops, just like how The Watchtower described worldly women. Taze thought of Akari, his uncle, Brother Simmons counsel, Brother Choker, his job, and a whole entire conglomeration of other topics and issues, not these worldly women. Horace, on the other hand, wanted to associate with them.

"So, ladies, how's your evening going?"

"Aren't you going to ask to buy us a drink?"

Taze thought, "That's exactly how the Watchtower describes bar life and the worldly women in it."

They got their drinks, and the ladies flirted.

One of them looked at Taze and asked, "What do you do for work?"

"Ah . . . well, I'm . . . ah . . . unemployed at the moment."

Horace interjected to help Taze, who didn't want any help. "Taze is on a sabbatical. He's actually a literature professor."

"Wow! He sounds smart, a professor."

"Actually, an adjunct professor."

About twenty minutes later Taze walked one of the worldly women to her car, and she gave him a hug. She got into her car and drove off. At that second, he noticed a car parked across the street with an older couple. He recognized the car from the Kingdom Hall parking lot. He yelled to himself, "No! It can't be. It can't be Brother and Sister Dandy." He looked closer. They looked back at him. He muttered, "Did they

31

follow me? Where did they come from? Did Horace set me up? Am I hallucinating?"

When he returned home, he noticed several messages. He thought, maybe Akari, maybe the elders, or maybe his aunt.

He ran toward the phone and listened to his voice mail:

Taze--Call me it's very urgent. It's about your uncle. What happened with your phone?

Taze—Call me now! Where are you?

Taze—Call now!

In every message he heard his aunt get more upset. Every message seemed to illustrate a message he'd been expecting for years.

Taze said to himself, "My uncle is dead. Now what? Has anything literally changed besides that singular fact? He died. Must it relate to my emotional state of being? I don't want to hear the news from my aunt because she'll talk at length about how he's coming back, and how he will be resurrected by Jehovah, and I'll see him again if I pledge allegiance to The Watchtower organization."

       *   *   *

"Mr. Felix, the doctor can see you now."

Taze walked to the backroom at the end of the hallway.

"So, Taze, where were we? Um . . . my notes say fifteen."
"Well, doctor, my uncle, he di . . ."
"Listen Taze. Let's just focus on your childhood. Can we focus, please?"

"Sure doctor . . . sure. It started with my religion. An oppressive religion, and it continued with the death of everyone that has ever meant anything to me. They all died either metaphorically, emotionally, or literally. They collapsed like stars or black holes or reverse black holes. They self-destructed. These were the people that meant everything for me . . . everything . . . every breath of my life, and where's the savior? Not some spiritual God savior . . . I mean a savior, a physical person, an actual entity, flesh, bones, knees, knuckles, nose, veins, capillaries, brains. I don't want the greasy food memories. I don't want the brick edifice of the Kingdom Hall. I don't want the literature counter. I don't want tall urinals or bathroom visits to pass time and gas. Listen, doctor! I need death. I need to die. I need to have my brain removed. I need unconsciousness because the wiseman Solomon said, 'The dead are conscious of nothing.' He was correct. And that was the only worthwhile thing I ever learned at Kingdom Hall. That was the only physical thing. The only thing I can bury or dig up or breathe out my nostrils."

"Mr. Felix, have you filled your prescriptions for Xanax and Prozac, yet? They will help you to calm down and stay focused. You have to find constructive ways to deal with your anxiety and depression."

*   *   *

"Brother Felix! We need to have some words with you tonight in the backroom after the meeting. It's very important."

Taze realized that he did not dream the events of the previous evening. He actually lived them. Brother and Sister Dandy actually saw him hug a worldly woman.

"Brother Felix, we wanted to speak with you concerning what Brother and Sister Dandy witnessed the other night outside The Speckled Toad Pub." He turned to Brother Choker, "It is the Speckled Toad Pub, right?" Brother Choker nodded.

"Well, Brother Felix, according to Brother and Sister Dandy, they said you were at this pub drinking heavily and cavorting with worldly women. These women." The elder presented a photo on his phone. "That's you, right?"

"Yes, that's me, but . . ."

"And those are worldly women, right?"

"I don't know. I really . . ."

"They look worldly. One has a tattoo and the other a nose ring."

"Well, yeah, they look worldly, but . . ."

"So, they're worldly, and those are drinks, and that's you, and it looks like you may have had about seven or eight drinks that we know of. There may have been more. Let me show you a scripture." The elder presented the scripture where Jehovah outlawed drunkenness for the Israelites and another scripture for the Christians.

"You see drunkenness alone is a serious matter, one that Jehovah can only forgive with true repentance, and it seems by the way you're reacting, that you are not truly repentant. In fact, I'm going to guess that you didn't even pray for forgiveness last night."

"Listen . . ."

"We love you, and Jehovah loves you. But this activity is like a bull running toward its own slaughter, and you ran toward that immorality. Is that you embracing that worldly woman?"

"Yes." Taze slumped down defeated. How could he win against the bible, these photos, and these elders? There was no argument, and Taze didn't care anyway.

*   *   *

"So, this will blow the head clean off a doe?"

"Sure will."

Taze found himself at a gun shop. Not a large sporting goods corporate gun shop, but a backwoods, middle of nowhere, no waiting period to buy a gun, gun shop.

"Yes, that's what I'd like to do, blow the head clean off a doe."

34

"How much?"

"$375, plus $50 for ammo."

"Right, ammo, right."

Taze looked around the glorified pawnshop. There hung camouflage shirts and jackets on every turn. There hung all sorts killing devices and all sorts of symbols of death. Pry the gun from my cold dead hand, confederate flag, kill the Yankee queers, the south will rise again, lynch 'um. Posters of large gruff men supporting the antlers of some defenseless creature. A creature that didn't ask to live or die. A creature that only wanted to be. Taze thought of the animals that were slaughtered in Noah's flood. "What is one life worth anyway?" he thought.

Taze continued to look around. Newspaper clippings of men proudly standing tall next to long giant sea creatures. A slogan read, "This is the newest way to catch the fish you want." Nothing but an advertisement. Just another way for death to beget death.

"How much, again?" Taze lost his concentration. He faded into memories, faded into his past. He saw himself holding hands with his uncle and singing from the old purple songbook. Other children flocked to his uncle, but none of those children had to save him from an alcohol and guilt induced suicide attempt. They never had to pick his limp and dead weight body out of the bathtub with urine, blood, and vomit squeezing through their fingers. Taze faded deeper into a memory with his uncle as they walked through a field of heavy deep grass with a tree filled mountain that stood lofty in the distance and with a special glow transfixed above its peak. They followed the path of a spring, a pure spring where they occasionally rested and tasted its water with clean innocent hands.

A sublimated fantasy in the pictures from The Watchtower publications that Taze stared at for hours during long weekly meetings.

They hiked up and never took their eyes off the peak. Strangely, they passed people who smiled and cut up fruits and harvested vegetables and painted pictures. His uncle looked down tall upon his young nephew and wiped a slight bead of sweat from his temple.

"Only a couple hundred feet left. The end is almost here," he said in a masculine and caring voice, a voice that sent comfort into Taze's heart. A voice that stood as high as the mountain they approached.
"There it is. There's that white hawk you told me about."
"Yes, it is. We will follow it to the top. Do you know what's at the very top of that mountain? Jehovah."

"$375 for the rifle, $50 for the ammo."
Taze regained focus. "Oh . . . ah . . . okay. Cash only, right?"
"Cash only son."
"Here it is." He handed it to the clerk with shaky hands, dirty and dry.
"You alright boy? Listen, son, I don't ask no questions, and I definitely don't answer any either."

*   *   *

Taze returned home and noticed a beautiful picture of his aunt and the rest of the family from a zoo visit at three years old. "This is fiction, this picture. This never happened. This is nothing. It is contrived. This never was. We are smiling. We are happy. We are together. Who thought of such an insane and immoral idea as to take such a photograph?" He focused on his aunt. "She was young and beautiful and healthy and happy. That's not true. She had her arm around my uncle and me. That's false. My cousin is waving. Completely untrue."

"Oh, Jehovah. I stand on the other side of life's waters stream."

Taze didn't dare look into any mirrors and avoided all of them by ducking or using separate hallways. He grabbed the end of the rifle. The trigger could easily be pulled while the other end rested on his teeth and tasting his tongue. He thanked Jehovah for long limbs. Limbs that could have helped him play basketball for the school team in a different childhood. He didn't write a note.

"Why should I have any last words? Let everybody else figure out the mystery on their own. They're the smart ones."

"What room should I do this in?" Taze thought about it for a minute and the image of The Watchtower version of Jesus pointing to a picture of a narrow open road leading to everlasting life entered his mind.

He chose the downstairs bathroom. Just a nice little purple room where blood could soak into purple rugs and his brain that held important memories could accidentally float in the toilet and traces of bone could rest in the tiny crevices of the linoleum tile. Where his arm could lay stiff on tissue boxes, and the fan could mute the smell. Taze pictured the explosion several times in slow motion, a piece of reality artwork. The artwork of depression. The true and final artistic masterpiece on the wall.

He held the rifle up perfectly. "God give me a reason not to do this!"

The phone rang. It sat right in front of him and displayed Akari's number.

"Hello."

"Hi, Taze. It's Akari. I heard about the sabbatical. What's wrong?"

"Oh . . . ah . . ."

"Well. What are you doing?"

Taze looked down at the rifle, "Nothing. Not much. You?"

"I broke up with my boyfriend. Do you want to get together tonight? I could use the company."

"Yes. Sure. Absolutely."

Taze put down the gun and went to his upstairs bathroom. He showered with lotions and shampoos with exotic sweet-smelling soaps from India. He shaved all over his body. He cleaned himself carefully making sure every bubble penetrated each pore.

He faced the mirror remembering his sadness for a moment but continued on, running olive oil through his hair and massaging his scalp with mousse and gel. His curly hair shined and after he shaved, he clipped his nose hairs and trimmed his eyebrows. He looked complete.

Tee shirt- the cleanest one without any sign or vestiges of sweat stains or yellowish armpit residue.

Boxers- blue plaid- no semen stains, no urine, and absolutely no diarrhea or symbol of past malaria, food poisoning or parasites. No blood either.

Socks- fancy- hand washed in sink-blue stripes on tan canvas. Spray with cologne

Shoelaces- matched perfectly with black leather shoes purchased in New York little Italy- square front- sleek sides, and cushioned soles burgundy strip- classy

Ribbed turtleneck black tight-beatnik- matched his hair and large framed glasses-flowed with Kerouac book in front pocket

Dark blue jeans- deep blue jeans

Ready.

Taze walked into his garage and started up his car. Before he pressed the button of the automatic garage door opener, he caught his reflection in the rear-view mirror. He could barely see a shadow of himself, just some curls. He saw a child.

Taze coughed and fell into a fantasy.

He saw his uncle behind a podium on a stage as he talked into a microphone. He saw a tall man who read the next paragraph in the Watchtower magazine. He saw brothers and sisters who raised their hands and read their answers. He saw a picture of paradise on page twelve with faces that smiled and the animals and the big garden homes and the fruits and vegetables and the sun that shone in the corner and the kids with lions and the adults carefree and then he saw himself in the rearview mirror and then . . . he blacked out.

Part 2- "Now's the time to…" (Mid-2006)

They had nine cats: Blinky, Dinky, Giovanni, Plinky, Linky, Mercucio, and three others. Two men in their late twenties who tried to live like libertarian heroes amidst the backdrop of a giant rural Walmart in the state of Virginia. They gave plenty of advice about cilium husk and horsetail juice or any other all-natural supplement. Denny Wister took care of the cats, worked six hours a month as an attorney, and smoked pot eight times a day. Horace Brewer, his stocky Jehovah's Witness housemate, ran a business and did his best to dodge the elders. He mainly tried to cleanse his colon.

Yes, they had nine cats who ran around, peed, and shit all over the house, a mountain villa with a view of the giant Walmart. Horace slept fifteen hours a day and ran his business that repaired wooden surfaces and said to clients, "We'll be there within a week," but he usually didn't get the job done. His undocumented workers always quit. At the same time, during the winter months, Denny kept the heat on ninety degrees, which forced Horace to open his bedroom window on thirty degrees nights.

Denny resembled Jehovah's original blueprint for the giraffe, a tall, almost albino man, with spots.

Horace resembled a 1994 version of Billy Joel with his hair receding in an earlier stage of evolution, as if Jehovah said, "I'll have the hair fall out from back to front," and even though he had perfect physical health, he continually dreamed up physical ailments.

Denny's daily hygiene consisted of one greasy swipe of an old plastic back pocket comb through his very long stringy hair. Horace used dozens of creams, lotions, herbal pills, husks, brillo pads, sponges, disks, and pucks that all laid out on the bathroom counter.

Denny bathed once a week in bubbles from former hotel shampoo plastic bottles. His sister gave him a collection from her job as cleaning manager of a fledgling Howard Johnsons.

"Listen, you have to turn down the temperature. It was thirty degrees outside last night, and I had to crack open a window."
"I don't want the cats to catch cold."
"How many more cats are we going to own? They're gonna start to mate soon, and I think Minkly shit on my pillow again." Horace pointed to a small brown feline ass print.
Denny calmly replied, "We don't own the cats; they own us."
"Where's my cilium husk?" Horace shouted.
"How am I supposed to know? I'm regular. I eat oatmeal every day,"

Denny ate instant oatmeal every day. His diet consisted of easy and fast to prepare vegetarian foods. He ate wheat germ, rolled oats, apple cider, organic apple cider vinegar, wheat, weeds, barks, ginger root, nutmeg, peas, hay, and random seeds.

Both men shielded themselves from the outside world. They sank into desperate depressions, but they held hope in private property and growing their own vegetables. They wanted to live free, away from taxes and government infringement, and they feared every trip away from their small mountain home. These poor guys rebelled against therapy, medical doctors, currency, and Federal Reserve notes. They wanted to be individuals.

Purchases

"Can we please get that hot tub finished, please?" asked Horace.

"Well, we need some tubing, some lubing, some artificial stone, a wooden platform, a circuit breaker, a wire, some glue, some nails and other tools and about one thousand dollars."

About a year earlier, Horace brought home a used hot tub. When they carried the hot tub frame and its small go-cart motor, they imagined nights of brisk coolly drinks with sixty-eight degree air and a breathtaking view of the Blue Ridge Mountains. Instead, it sat near the shack in the backyard amidst the weeds and brush.

Horace also bought two old vans. Denny needed a crane, an engine lifter, air compressed tools and all sorts of other things before could even start to fix them.

One night they drove to the worst part of Richmond looking at a van at 11:41pm. They intended to arrive at around eight and even called the gentleman to confirm, but things didn't go as planned. Horace sat on the toilet and wished for a bowel movement, and Denny, with his OCD, filed the long end of a tiny screwdriver. He neatly and precisely took the metal shavings and placed them in a sandwich baggie that held shavings from times past and said to himself, "Someday the world will need metals, and I'll have them."

A burly black man answered the door.

He said angrily, "I don't do business like this!"
Horace tried to reason with the man, "But can't we just see the van. We got lost, please?"

"I don't do business like this."

A woman from the back yelled out, "Hey Marv, who's that?"

Marv responded, "Some couple a smart asses want to see the van, but I don't do business like that."

"Listen," Horace spoke up as Denny looked on timidly, "We just want to take a look at the van, and we don't come to the city very often. Please."

They rarely ventured into the city. They lived up in the mountains about fifty miles away.

"Please, sir."

"No, get your asses home."

Later that week on a small farm in an even more rural part of Virginia, they arrived four hours early at five thirty in the morning to see a different van.

"Who the hell is that?"

"Just a couple a Yankees wanttin' to see that ole van we got rustin' up in those weeds."

"Please sir, can we take it for a test drive, please?"

"You know what time it is? You woke me up!"

"Please sir, we just want to see the van and take it for a quick test drive."

"Get your asses outta here 'fore I get my shotgun."

Clean Deck

Horace waited on the phone for somebody to pick up when he yelled to Denny, "There's cat urine in the corner." The person answered, and Horace focused on his phone call, "Hi there, this is Horace Brewer from Clean Deck, and I believe you called regarding an estimate on your deck. We're going to be in the area this week, so . . ."

"Oh. I called you ten days ago for that estimate. Sorry, but I went with somebody else."

43

Horace threw his phone while Denny saved the seeds from a tangelo that he'd been peeling for the previous thirty-seven minutes.

Denny wore the same sweatshirt every day. The gray stripe on his sweatshirt stuck out straight like a Florida canal across the Everglades. Somehow it provided a sense of nourishment to Denny. Horace bought him a three pack of plain white undershirts and a sharpie magic marker and told Denny to write anything he wanted to write on the shirts. Instead, the package sat at the bottom of a teeter tauter contraption Denny used to lay upside down. It collected enough dust for a robust colony of mites to prosper. The marker dried up like the Euphrates in an uninterruptible Pharisee nightmare.

Horace penned a new colonic poem:

Oh cilium husk
I trust
Thee to make colon clean and
Free and unclog the fog of
Mind that cheese and heavy stuffing
Bind like tree of Daniel in
Prophetic verse
Please make it the first
Part of the day
With coffee on tray
Suppository on shelf
let spinach resemble Atlantic kelp
As I examine it whole or floating in parts
Praying thankfully and lustfully for
Eternal
Organic
Farts

Horace still obsessed over his ex-girlfriend, Maribella, an undocumented and worldly Mexican woman who cashed his checks at a gas station after Horace refused to use banks. Horace still visited Maribella at the gas station even after she started to date a normal machismo Mexican man. Horace wanted to get back together with Maribella, but he knew the difficulties he faced during their two-year unevenly yoked courtship, like the language barrier, and the unfortunate time she caught him masturbating to a legs and feet fetish website.

*   *   *

Horace set up his business so that his customers paid the undocumented workers directly. This required him to provide a convoluted explanation to the suburban white homeowners of Richmond, already predisposed to be leery of non-white people.

"So, who do I make the check out to?"
"Well, sir, we have several payment options." His only options:

Pay the undocumented worker.
Pay in gold or silver.

"Go ahead and pay the worker that does the job at your house in cash. If you want to pay by check, just make the check out to whoever does the job."
"What sort of guarantee do I have?"

He didn't have one, so Horace used his elaborate communication skills, mainly learned from the Theocratic Ministry School, to explain this concept gently.

"Well, that's a fantastic question! If you have any issues at all, you can call this number (Horace ignored that number) or you can call the worker directly (his workers didn't have phones) and it's all backed up by Clean Deck (it wasn't. legally there was no Clean Deck, and no mention of the term was ever put in writing) and . . ."

"So, how do I make an appointment?"

Horace never made appointments. His workers went where he told them to go, regardless of their schedules or the homeowners' schedules.

"We'll be out your way within a couple days . . . a week at most, and you don't have to be home when we arrive, but if you want to you can. Leave payment under your doormat or in a safe place."
"Can you give me a call before you come?"
"Sure, no problem." He never did. Clean Deck paralleled his own constant state of depression and anxiety. Nonetheless, it still stood as a masterful achievement for Horace.

* * *

"Mr. Baltimore. I'm Deputy Levi Edmunds from the Chesterfield County Sheriff's Department, and I have a few questions for you."
"Ah . . . this is ah . . . not Robert Baltimore. This is Ferguson Schmedly."
"According to my information and by matching voices, you are most definitely Mr. Robert Baltimore, and you need to take down your Clean Deck signs from the sides of all our roads immediately. We have photographic evidence of you putting signs out. We've asked you several times to remove those signs."
"Ah . . . this is Ferguson Schmedly."

Horace mainly advertised through the use of thousands of signs plastered all over the metro Richmond area and all the sheriff's departments tried to find either Robert Baltimore, Rick Gunn, Ferguson Joe, Ferguson Schmedly, Rich Stadium, Minneapolis Visp, or one of the many aliases he utilized to avoid judgment. He owned four beepers, two cell phones, and two landlines for Clean Deck. The voicemail greetings consisted of messages like, "Hi, this is Rick Gunn of Quest Marketing, please leave us your name, number, the address of the home you'd like estimated,

46

and I'll get right back to you" or "Good afternoon. I'm Minneapolis, and I'll get a contractor for you right away."

Every time the police called, Horace threw a tantrum and spent days in bed and moaned, "What I am going to doooooooooo?" He'd shake in the bed for hours.

Days Past

Of course, the story of these two men started a long time before they moved in together. In fact, they didn't even meet until just before they moved in together. They had a mutual childhood friend, Taze Felix, who introduced them. Taze grew up with and befriended both Horace and Denny in Cleveland, but Horace and Denny never met.

As it goes, Denny grew up in a hyper-scientifically organized suburban family. Everything in the house had a place perfectly measured with rulers, balances, tape measures, and whatever mathematical equation essential for perfection. Whether hanging a picture on the wall of a first communion or storing used twist ties, everything had a place, an order, a time, a pattern, and his family knew it and practiced it and forced it on Denny. Denny's father worked as an accountant and volunteered as a Boy Scout troop leader. He knew every knot and how to earn every merit badge. A Vietnam Vet and a meticulous beer drinker who took tiny sips every night until he drank exactly six beers. Sometimes during Browns football games, he drank eight. A small man, thin, with long straight dark black hair that hung down over his ears. Genuine and real, he referred to Denny, his only son, simply as "The Asshole."

When a young Taze knocked on his door and innocently asked, "Is Denny home?" Mr. Wister always responded, "The asshole will be out in a

47

minute." Quiet and mild mannered but unfortunately angry all the time because of his trauma from Vietnam. Denny's mother encouraged him to pursue academics and horn instruments. She filled in his Ohio University application and even wrote the entrance essay. She made Denny play an obscure brass instrument called the euphonium because it made his application stand out.

"Denny! Denny! Shovel the snow in the driveway and pick that ice!" His father obsessively made sure that no presence of snow or ice appeared on their driveway during the winter. During the eight months of snowfall and winter temperatures, literally every inch and crevice of the driveway had to be cleared of snow and ice.

Horace's childhood: Paper route, trendy clothes, a spoon looking object to keep his penis straight while he peed, constant Jehovah's Witness meetings and field service for The Watchtower, plenty of masturbation, and guitar playing,

His sarcastic father drank whisky with his anti-depressant meds. He demanded Horace have a strong presence in the congregation. His father married young and had a son that Horace never met. Horace longed to meet his older brother, but he was disowned and lived with his mother. Horace's mother, an excellent cook, acted depressed much of the time, especially with Horace around. Horace never learned proper social skills. They told Horace 974 times between the ages of 3 and 12 that he would live forever on a paradise earth and that he would never grow old. Horace realized at about 25, that he would get old, and that he would most definitely die.

A Day in the Life: The Elders Visit Horace

Denny woke up one morning alarmed by a distant moan, "Ahhggg . . . ahhhggg." Horace performed his morning ritual of extreme moaning. "Ahhhggg." Denny heard it again. He hated it on this particular morning because he officially fell asleep at 6:55am, and the moans started at 7:12am.

As he attempted to block out the irritating noise, he wondered, "Oh, oh, maybe I should smoke a bowl." Suddenly, a knock came on the front door and with Denny's deflated air mattress very close to the door, he could see the figure of a fifty-seven-year-old man named Roy. Roy talked with a heavy accent, the kind nobody could figure out. Maybe he's American with a speech infirmity or maybe he's Hungarian. Nobody knew.

So, Denny pretended to sleep, and Roy walked right in and headed toward the sound of the grunts. "Come on Horace! Don't you know we have an 8 o'clock appointment?" Horace often made plans with others, particularly for Clean Deck but failed to follow through.

"Come on sleepy head! Wake up! Get your ass outta bed. We have an 8 o'clock together, an estimate in Tuckahoe and two in Petersburg. Let's go." Horace rolled over and threw a cat off the bed. "I can't. The damn cat shit on my pillow again. He shit on my pillow again. Damn cat! I think it was Mercutio."

Roy helped himself to some cereal and asked about the milk.
"The milk is in the cupboard above the fridge."
"Above the fridge?"
"Yes. You need to add some water to it. It's powdered milk."

Roy took a hand full of cereal and ate some, "Come on. Let's go!"

"Ahhggg," Horace stumbled to the kitchen and another visitor arrived. A seventeen-year-old naïve looking guitar toting kid, ready to smoke some weed at the only place besides his car available. Denny quickly rolled off the deflated airless mattress.

That specific mattress used to be able to hold air, but one of the cats scratched it during a terrible fit and popped a hole small enough to allow tiny squeaks of air to flow out at a pace that Denny later calculated as twelve air particles per second, or in more practical terms, if Denny inflated the mattress right before he went to bed, he'd get about five hours of somewhat comfortable sleep, but that was a big *if* for Denny because sometimes his apathy led him to just plop down on the deflated mattress. Once and while Denny remembered the moment he received the mattress, a gift from his father just before a Boy Scout camping retreat in New Mexico. He remembered how his father said it was cactus proof and could withstand a variety of prickers, spines, and spikes. A short slight memory of the New Mexico trip included Denny's discovery of two Mormon scoutmasters involved in sexual activity, but that was fifteen years ago and maybe the rubber had lost its strength, lost its will and so a measly cat claw ruined it.

"Aloha," whistled Denny.
"Still no sofas? That's cool," said the teen.

Horace overheard and chimed in, "We're getting them today from Jean Braselton." Right after he made this statement, he realized the implications, "AHHHHH shit, I can't do those estimates today. Can you do them Roy, pllleeese?" whimpered Horace. Then he came to the realization that the teens visited for the sole purpose of smoking weed. This upset Horace, and he ran back to his bedroom. Roy caught only a quick glimpse of his extra tight burgundy and gold boxer briefs.

A gigantic fart sent waves of a sickly scent through the house. The sound of Horace's cell phone and a gasp, "It's Braselton. You answer it, Denny," he ran out of the room and handed the phone to Denny,
"No, you answer. I'm not your secretary." Nobody answered the phone.
It rang again. "Answer it, pllleeese," cried Horace.
"No, I don't need a new sofa."
"It's not new. I'm getting a good deal on it from Braselton. I'm just not prepared to speak right now."
"AHHHH!" The phone flew in the air as beeps announced a new voice mail. The beeps resounded in five-second intervals. Denny calculated this almost instantly. Horace noticed this fact the moment Denny's face froze. It occurred during second number three between beep number four and five. Somehow the message played aloud. Apparently, the speakerphone option turned on when Horace threw his phone, and a squeaky voice with a Lake Erie accent confidently echoed through the hallways:

"Hi, Horace. Jean Braselton here. Me, Dawn and the kids are gonna to be scootin' up your way in about (pause) four hours with those sofas. We're bringing lunch, so don't worry about that . . . well . . . you could pick up some pop if you want. Travis likes cherry . . ." (beep)

Another beep signified the end of the message cutting off the drink order. Horace programmed his phone to record messages for only ten seconds because of the innumerable phones calls that flowed in for Clean Deck. More messages played for everyone to hear.

"This is the third message I left today. Again, I am Don Hazelton and I live at 1864 S Sycamore Street in Petersburg. I wanted to confirm our appointment for an estimate on my back deck . . . but now you can take your Clean Deck and shove it up my clean . . ." (beep)

"Horace, WAKE UP! It's Roy, get your ass outta bed . . ." (beep)

"Hey guy, Jean here. Give me a call back. Wanted to touch base with you about that sofa set." (beep)

"This is Don Hazelton, and this my second phone call today. You said you'd be in my neighborhood today, and I wanted to confirm my estimate appointment. Please get back to me before I decide to . . ." (beep)

"Hello Brother Brewer. Brother Michael Beagley here. We haven't seen you at any meetings in a few weeks, and we wanted to know if you'd like a visit of encouragement from Brother Collar and myself. You can get back to me on that. One more thing, Sister Barlabin said she saw some teenagers smoking inside your house. She said the smoke smelled like mari . . ." (beep)

"Horace, how many times do I have to call you? Have you been to the meetings lately? I hope so." (His mother)

Everyone in the house stood like newly embalmed corpses and listened intently to each message. Something struck the listeners. Was it a sense of sympathy that the pothead teenager suddenly felt? Did Denny feel a moment of remorse for not answering the phone? Was Roy trembling from Don Hazelton's curt tone? All of them received a tiny glimpse into Horace Brewer's life. Thirty seconds later the others resumed their activities. Denny and the teen rolled a joint. Roy left, and Horace adjusted his burgundy briefs and scratched the hair directly above his crotch.

After the scratch, Horace used his percolator to make some coffee. He drank half a cup. Then, he felt a slight rumble near the bottom of his stomach. This excited him immensely and before he even entered the unintentionally retro seventies decorated bathroom, he pulled down his burgundy briefs just past his kneecaps. He always kept a notebook on the crown of the yellow toilet just behind his arched back. He kept the notebook there in case a moment of colon inspired poetry hit him and, on that day, it did.

Poem:
Slip sliding away
Through Bowery bowel
Like a broken subway car
During giant big apple power outage
A constipated Kerouac
A gassy Ginsberg
A chocolate Bukowski

He stopped writing for a moment as water splashed upward misting the hairs on both sides of his crack. A tiny drip slid off one particularly curly hair and dropped back into the bowl. Plinky, sensitive to the slight sound, let out a childish meow. Denny interpreted it as a cry for food.

"Plinky, do you want a treat, a small can of special feast?" Plinky did not respond, but Denny continued speaking in a cutesy voice, "Do you want some water? You're a silly cat!"

Horace stared down at the yellow triangular tiles and lost momentum. He pushed and squeezed, but nothing happened. He gave up on his new poem. This disheartened him, and he trudged back to his bed and fell back asleep.

Denny began smoking marijuana from a homemade gravity bong, which led to an intense conversation with the teen that seemed significant and immensely profound.

"Whoa, how did you make that Denny?" asked the teen pothead.

The teen asked the question with such vigor and enthusiasm that a half asleep and incredibly depressed Horace heard and thought, "Oh no. Here it comes." He knew that Denny would supply a long drawn out, overly technical, scientific explanation to the pothead teen. Horace thought, "He'll suck the life out of that kid with his answer."

Denny began, "Well, ah . . . ah, let me show you. This is a giant cast iron pot my grandmother retrieved from Poland in 1974. She . . . ah . . . gave it to me as gift for making Eagle Scout. You have to use cast iron. It can't be any other metal because it holds heat at twelve degrees higher for twice as long as . . . let's say . . . an aluminum pot. Also, their iron handles provide an important carrier of heat, whereas some of the new stew pots have plastic handles held in by cheap screws, usually with Phillips head."

Horace heard all of this, forced to listen because of Denny's excited elevated voice. He only wished for peace, tranquility, and transcendence to sleep.

Denny continued as the teen sat mesmerized. "So, you take a giant cast iron pot about sixteen inches deep. Make sure the bottom is smooth and, if you have to, use a small wire brush to smooth out the rough spots. Use a level. Never use sandpaper unless it is the very lightest grade of coarseness. Fill the pot three quarters of the way or twelve inches from the bottom with tap water at room temperature. It must be room temperature."

A strong knock on the door interrupted Denny's glowing explanation. Two Alfred Hitchcockesque silhouettes stood outside holding briefcases. Horace's eyes opened. He wiped drool off his mouth and felt frightened. Denny confirmed his fear as he completely abandoned his treatise: "Of Gravity Bong" and shouted to Horace, "Horace! Horace! It's a couple of old guys from your Kingdom Hall."

"Ugh. What do they look like?"

"They're both obese and bald. One has some severe razor burn, and the other is wearing a clip-on tie. It looks like the slightly fatter guy hasn't shined his shoes in a decade."

"Shit."

The unkempt shoes gave it away. Brother Michael Beagley, visiting with "encouragement." At that moment, it started to rain.

Denny let the obese elders inside only to annoy Horace. Immediately, Brother Beagely's large, enflamed nostrils contracted with contemptuous energy. Then he glanced quickly to the other fat man, Brother Collar, and nodded while his dangling chin flapped one step behind and whispered, "Smells like grass."

"Hi there, Denny. Is Horace available?"

Denny quickly said, "Yes, I'll get him." He walked down the short hall, to the backroom and opened the door. He also stepped with one bare foot onto some tweezers covered in cat shit.

"Horace, your Jehovah Witness elders are here to encourage you." Horace stumbled from the bed and walked to the living room.

"Hello, Brother Brewer," said Brother Beagley. Brother Collar nodded and said, "We were in the neighborhood visiting Brother Chuck Knox, so we thought we'd stop by and talk for ten minutes. Can we have a seat?"

"Sure," said Horace begrudgingly.

"So, Brother Brewer. How have you been?"

"Oh, I'm okay. I've had a little cold for a few days. Just trying to get over it." He coughed.

"A cold. Well, we're sorry to hear that. You know, Brother Braids has been in chemo for three weeks and hasn't missed a meeting. He even prayed the other night."

"Oh, well, yeah, um, he is a fine brother."

"I'm a straight shooter. So, I'll shoot straight. It seems like you've been toting the line lately with your conduct, association, and attitude, in general. Do you realize that bad associations spoil useful habits? In fact, let's look at that scripture. Do you have your bible handy?"

Horace walked into his bedroom, head down, and searched intensely for his Bible. It was an early nineteen seventies hard cover green edition with his name etched in gold leaf on the bottom left-hand corner. It was a baptism gift from his parents ten years earlier. They read the scripture together. Just behind the skin of Horace's forehead, his skull trembled intensely. He thought he could feel the fixed joint of his skull separate like crusts of adjoining land under ocean waters.

"It seems that you're missing a lot of meetings. I noticed that you've missed twenty-three of the last thirty-one meetings, most of which are on Thursday night, and the Sunday meetings you've attended, you've left early every time. Why is this?"

"I've been busy."

"Too busy for Jehovah and his banquet of spiritual food?"

"Well, I've been under stress from . . ."

"If you come to the meetings, that stress will disappear."

56

"But you don't understand. The meetings give me stress."

"WHAT! The Kingdom Hall is a place of refuge from Satan's world."

"My parents . . ."

"Listen, we could all blame our parents. My parents were Catholic. Now what could be worse than that?"

Brother Collar piped in, "Did your parents ever force you to speak in tongues? Mine did."

"No, but . . ."

"Your parents raised you the right way. Read this, it says, 'Do not forsake the gathering of yourselves for to incite to fine works.' Do you know what incite means? It means to sharpen. I sharpen you; you sharpen me."

As much as Horace wanted to rejoice in that reciprocal formula, and as much as he admired the behemoth eloquence that sprayed from the elder's mouth, he couldn't agree. His central nervous system wouldn't let him. Neither would his colon. But he complied.

"I'll be at the next meeting. You can count on it."

"Well, that's just fine, Brother Brewer."

Horace thought the visit was over and was about to thank the elders and walk them to their cars.

But it wasn't over.

"One more thing Brother Brewer." An uncomfortable energy fogged the room along with the residual pot smoke. Just as Brother Beagley began to speak, Horace's phone rang. Horace rarely answered his phone, but out of desperation, he did. He saw the caller ID: Brother Jean Braselton.

"Hello."

"Hey guy, it's Jean Braselton. I should be there with the sofas in about two and half hours. I just have to take Dawn to a garage sale. She found a wooden stool for seven dollars, talked the lady down to four seventy-five. Also, Travis needs a new repair kit for his glasses. The rain is a little heavy, so if you could pick up some plastic sheets that would help. Oh . . . and . . . do you have a grill? I'm bringing burgers."

"No, ahh . . ."

"Well, the burgers are on ice, so if you could pick one up, lunch is on me."

"I'll see."

Somehow the phone disconnected, and the visit of "encouragement" continued.

"Where were we, Brother Brewer? Oh, yes, several of the brothers and sisters in the neighborhood have noticed some unsightly smells and some unpleasant company here at your house. You know Brother . . . I'm a frank person. I'll come right out and tell you. Your house smells like grass, and there seems to be a slew of young longhaired teens going in and out. Are you trafficking grass?"

The three brothers heard a bubbling noise from the other room.

Horace's mind returned to The Watchtower conversation in front of him. He nervously replied, "I don't traffic drugs, Brother Beagley."

Brother Beagley responded, "Well, we can't prove it, unless we have two witnesses who actually see you sell the grass, but if you want a clear your conscience, call us. Well, that just about does it. Let's say a prayer together."

Horace sat between the two obese elders and the three held hands in a circle.

In his thick southern accent Brother Collar prayed:

Jehovah God, we come humbly before you in prayer to ask you to please keep our congregation, your holy place of worship, clean. We ask that you forgive our sins because we do fall short, and we know that if we confess our sins, and are repentant, that you will forgive us. We offer you this prayer through the name of your son and our repurchaser, Jesus Christ. Ahmen.

"Okey Dokey. We have another visit to make, so we'll see you tomorrow."

Horace nodded slowly in agreement .

The two elders left the house. Horace walked over to the window and looked out. As Brother Collar closed his umbrella, Horace heard Brother Beagley say into his phone, "I'll be home in an hour Linda. Got to go talk to Sister Heath . . . another pedophile case."

*   *   *

Brother Jean Braselton, Ministerial Servant, sells <u>Horace his Old Sofa Set</u>

Horace and Denny went to the Walmart. Denny filled half their cart up with cat food and cat litter. Denny had no money to pay for the cats, so Horace looked at his wallet with a glazed curiousness and wondered if it held enough cash. He had no credit card, only cash and some gold and silver hidden in old spaghetti sauce jars.

"Excuse me," said Horace to an employee, "Where are the grills?"
"You lookin' at em' son."

They sat directly in front of his face. Discouraged and belittled, he approached the least expensive grill, $19.00, but Denny quickly pointed out the flaws of the metal. "This type of aluminum will start to warp far before correct cooking temperature." Then, Horace grabbed the next step up, a $27.00 grill, but again Denny found a flaw. "See these plastic wheels, they won't hold up in any type of storm, so if you're planning on getting this one, we'll need a cover." The covers cost more than the grill. Thunder from outside interrupted their conversation.

"Whoa," said Denny. "We need to hurry, I think Mercucio is outside." Horace made an executive decision and looked Denny square in the eye, "We are getting this grill." Then, they bought charcoal, some lettuce, barbeque sauce, and a cucumber. Another twenty minutes passed. "Ahhh . . . it's Braselton again." The text message read:

Hey guy, it's Jean here. I'm at your house. I'm actually . . . ahh . . . in your house. Somebody named Camron let me in. It . . . ahhh . . . smells like pot in here, and I got a little worried. Anyway, I got the sofas. I'll wait here for ya, but Travis has to wait in the car because of his asthma.

Horace's phone beeped with another text message:

FYI- Burgers are in the fridge, looks like it's clearing up a bit.

They stood in a long line. A little girl behind them screeched and shrieked. Horace's temples exploded. Each button the cashier punched, pinched his spinal cord. Each word in the hillbilly conversations around him throbbed his temples. He felt intense pain when he finally got to the register and the bill came to $127.54. Then, Denny reminded him to get a plastic cover for the sofas to protect them from the rain. Horace thought about the excruciating process of getting out of the line, carting around all the stuff through the store to the back corner that seemed to stand a mile away, only to get some plastic to cover up sofas that Brother Jean Braselton pressured him into buying. He pictured seeing the men in the denim overalls, the jewelry counter ladies, the greaser section and the paint mixer, the tires and basketballs, the fishing rods and rifles, the fabric, the roasted chickens, the boneless skinless chicken breasts, the processed cheese crackers, he just couldn't do it. He stayed in line and paid for the items and even spoke up to Denny, "You know, you seem to always know and remember everything. Why couldn't you have told me about the plastic earlier?" And with that comment a massive bolt of lightning lit up the stormy sky and reflected off Denny's glasses.

It drizzled as they walked to the car, and Denny suggested the possibility of hail or a power surge at the house. The phone beeped again with another text message that seemed to display a slight bit of impatience and Great Lakes anger.

WHERE ARE YOU? Travis can't breathe so well.

"Braselton again?"
"Yes."
"Do you have the six hundred and fifty dollars to pay him for those sofas?"
"I have the cash. Except I only have hundreds. I hope he has change."

On the way home Denny noticed something small and frightened near the edge of the road. Horace thought to himself, "Oh no . . . not another cat!" The car stopped, and the passenger door opened. A strange catcall, original to Denny, came out of his mouth. The noise always irritated Horace, but every single cat always responded. The little shorthaired gray tabby walked slowly and suspiciously to Denny's safe embrace. They now had ten cats.

"Can we go back to the store?" asked Denny, "Looks like this little guy needs to be fed with a baby bottle."

"No, we don't have time," Horace responded. "Braselton is waiting with the sofas, and his spoiled brat son is coughing in their car, and it's raining again, and I bought a grill I will never use after today, and the damn elders are spying on me, and your druggy friends are smelling up our house, and I have three more messages from Don fucking Hazelton!"

They pulled into the driveway to see Brother Jean Braselton's fifty-thousand-dollar. Jean, a short thin gaunt man with thinning hair, approached Horace with a big handshake and smiled. Behind that smile, Jean housed the greedy thought that he purchased a sofa set six years earlier for less money than what Horace will pay for it six years later. Jean moved out of Cleveland, poor and hopeless, and started a million-dollar business in Virginia.

Horace thought, "Why does this guy want to cook hamburgers so bad?" Horace still hadn't eaten anything that day. He hadn't showered. He hadn't shit or shaved. His hair was a balding mess. He wore pleated short shorts. The bottom of his boxer briefs almost made it down past the bottom of his shorts.

"Hi, Jean."
"Hey sport, long time no see, you look great."
"Thanks. Where's the family?"
"Well, the wife saw a yard sale down the road, so I dropped her off. She has the girls with her. Travis is in the car watching a movie. Did you know that the best time to go to yard sales is on rainy days like this? You can get a steal on anything. Let's get those sofas under plastic."

Just as Jean pronounced the "c" in plastic the rain came down harder.

"I didn't get the plastic, maybe . . ."

"Well, I guess were gonna have to let them get a little wet. Let's hurry."

Jean was eager. In the meantime, Denny smoked a giant joint with Cameron and another teen. The teens stuck around when they heard about the burgers. Jean asked Denny to help them carry the love seat, while Horace and Jean's puny son, Travis, carried ends of the longer heavier lumpy green sofa.

"Okay Travis. Do you have it on your side?" Horace asked.

"Yes. Why are you growing corn in your front yard?" Travis asked.

"Are you sure you have it?" repeated Horace.

"Yes. I am sure."

Within three seconds, the sofa started to slide out of Travis's hand, and the rain fell even harder and soaked into the fabric. Travis dropped his end, slipped, and scraped his knee. A sprinkling of blood splashed onto the armrest.

The love seat already sat in the house and absorbed the smell of pot smoke. Jean ran outside when he heard his son squeal. "Trav! Trav! Are you okay champ?" The kid cried and blamed it on Horace. "He was carrying it too fast." He pointed at Horace and said weeping, "He dropped it on me." The rain continued to soak into the sofa. Denny slowly walked out of the house and, finally, they carried it in. The next instant the rain clouds passed. The rain stopped, and a bright sunshine appeared.

Slinky, the new cat, had some shit on its leg. Denny said, "Oooo . . . oooo, we're gonna have to give him a bath. In fact, I should give all the cats a bath."

Jean left for a moment to go pick up his wife and daughters. Travis decided to help wash the cats. Horace started to assemble the grill. He took all the pieces out of the box. He sighed and groaned. Quickly, he noticed two silver poles that could be attached on sight alone. "This piece must fit into this piece," he said to himself. Giovanni, the only outdoor cat of the bunch, walked up to Horace and gave him a friendly hello. This lightened his mood. He calmed down. As he turned around to reach for more pieces, a gentle breeze brought the powerful scent of the male feline in heat. When Horace picked up the directions they melted in his hand. "Denny!" he screamed, "DENNY!!"

Denny explained to Travis how to wash a cat. "You use a three- and half-inch bristle . . ." He heard the yell from outside. Travis's face held a look of wonderment. Denny shouted, "What?" Horace yelled in, "Giovanni sprayed on the grill instructions. They're ruined!"

Denny ran outside onto the patio to confirm. "Well, I'll have to go on the Internet and see if I could download some instructions. But I have to finish bathing six more cats first."

Horace decided to start constructing the salad but had to use the kitchen sink intermittently between cat soapings and rinsing. The cats hated baths. Each one screeched violently. Some scratched. Denny talked them down, "Now . . . now . . . be a good kitty. This is for your health. Only six percent of the world's felines get bathed regularly, and you're one of them."

Jean entered, "Hey guys, we're back . . . is lunch ready yet?" Just as Jean approached the kitchen Linky took a dangerous swing at Travis's forearm and a two-inch cut, straight as the equator, seeped with bright red blood. Five or six drops of it landed on some radishes in the sink. The wimpy kid let out a shriek of terror. Jean ran over.

Horace had no medical supplies whatsoever. Not a single band-aid. On the paper towel spindle only a couple centimeters of width remained. "Ahh, ahh . . . Ahhh. It stings and burns," Travis cried.
"Oh, Travis, you'll be alright." Jean comforted his son and yelled to his wife, "Dawn! Dawn! Do we have his blood card?"
"No! I left it in my other purse."

Panic saturated the house. Then the teenager, Camron, ran to his house to get some ointment and band-aids.

Travis stopped crying when promised ten dollars. He looked over at the torn lettuce pieces and allowed his mind to explore the possible jokes. Then, out it came, in a voice that still held some painful whimpering, "Those leaves look like kites." The entire room exploded in laughter. Each person, Denny, Jean, his wife, their two daughters, the stoner teenagers, even Travis himself, burst with laughter. All of them took looks at each other. They connected on some level of humor and let go of their inhibitions for a moment, to enjoy a medium range joke from a geeky, pale, nerdy spoiled kid.

Horace alone stood motionless. He drifted his vision to the low "do it yourself" popcorn ceiling. The laughter gradually lowered its level, and Jean's soft artist hand ran itself through his son's white hair and, while he looked into the crooked glasses, said with encouragement, "You're gonna be just fine. Now let's get this barbeque going."

All the people started to get busy on a project. Horace went to lay down in bed.

Denny took charge of the actual grilling. He loaded it up with charcoal and covered each piece with about an ounce of lighter fluid. Then he used a long lighter that he lengthened with some minor welding. It exploded and a frightened Travis jumped. Jean brought out the pre-shaped burger patties and threw them on the grill.

Denny tapped the side of one burger with a spatula. "Still a nice color and consistency, still not burnt," he thought. Travis stared into the fire mesmerized by the several different shades of orange. He said to Denny, "Usually dad cooks these for seven and half minutes. He even uses a timer that beeps." Then he made the noise, "BEEP . . . BEEP . . . BEEP." He jumped in place, like skipping rope without the rope. Making the connection to the beep noise, Horace picked his head up off the mattress and saw the boy out his bedroom window. His phone hadn't made any noises in fifteen full minutes. As he laid in bed on his stomach, Horace decided to leave his room and talk to his guests.

"Hey, Jean," Horace said.
Jean looked back surprised, "Horace, where have you been? We thought you pooped out on us?"
"No, I just had to use the phone."
"Thought maybe you were tired from helping Travis carry that sofa in."
"No, I just had to make a phone call."

Jean looked at his youngest daughter and smiled.

"You almost broke Travis's back with that sofa."
"Listen, Jean. I was in the bedroom for fifteen minutes making a short phone call. I am not tired. I am fine." Jean sat down as Horace exited to the patio.

Jean approached Dawn, nudging her, "I'm gonna ask him for forty more bucks."

Horace humbly walked over to the boys grilling,
"Maybe you should turn those over Denny?"
"They're not quite ready yet."
"Seriously, they should be turned over."
"One more minute."

Then, Denny made Travis's day by asking the boy to flip the burger. He handed him the spatula. Travis eagerly took it and vigorously slid it under one of the burgers. It took a little extra effort because the meat stuck to the grate. The three of them looked and saw a burnt, black, and charred burger.

"They burnt the hamburgers, daddy," yelled Travis.

Around the table, Horace looked at each person like in the commune scene from *Easy Rider*. Jean, Travis, Dawn, the two daughters, Denny, Camron, and the other two teen stoners. Jean broke when he asked Horace to say a prayer before the meal. He smiled and nudged Horace, "You're ain't D'F'ed, are ya?" Horace hadn't prayed out loud in at least three years. He started:

Oh Jehovah God, we thank you for this meal and this food. Um. Um. Um. Thank you for the fellowship of our brothers and um, um, others. Please forgive for our sins. Through Christ Jesus' name, Ahmen.

"What's for lunch papa?" one of the daughters asked.
"From what it looks like, burnt hamburgers and lettuce leaves that look like kites."
"Boy Horace, this is quite a spread," said Jean mockingly.
"Let me make some juice," said Denny.

Denny got up from the table to grab some beets, carrots, and celery. He threw them in his industrial contraption. Its grinding noise drowned out all the

conversation. When the juicer stopped Jean said,
"Hey Horace, maybe we can square up now?"
"Sure, you said six hundred fifty dollars."
"Well . . . now I'm thinking more like six ninety
because we delivered it."

Horace handed him the seven one-hundred-dollar bills.
Jean only returned a smug smile and a goodbye with
his trademark Lake Erie accent. Horace looked at the
giant vehicle as it pulled out of his driveway. He
looked behind him at the shitty worn green fabric of
the sofas and saw Plinky peeing in the center of the
center cushion.

*   *   *

Not too long after, Horace moved out of the house he
shared with Denny and put most of his stuff into a low
cost, low security storage unit. One morning, at a
vegan diner, he received a phone call.

"Hello."
"Hi Horace, I hate to be the bearer of bad news, but
your storage unit was broken into yesterday.   I went
over there to see what they took, and I don't think
they took anything."
"What about the sofas?"
"The sofas are still there."

Horace felt violated but, more so, humiliated. He
realized that even a band of thieves refused to steal his
only possessions.

About four weeks later, he found a tiny bedroom to
rent in a house of tweekers and residual cat fleas. He
hadn't talked to Jean since he bought the sofas. Then,
Jean called him out of the blue.

"Hey guy, how are ya?"
"Fine, just fine . . . how are you?"

"Good. Me and the kids are having a cookout over here, and we sure as heck would like ya to come?"
"Sure Jean. That sounds like fun. What time?"
"How about seven thirty?"
"Okay. I'll be there. Should I bring anything?"
"Nothing . . . it's all taken care of."

Maybe Jean Braselton wasn't such a heartless and arrogant Ministerial Servant after all. Maybe he was offering up his home and food and the company of his wife and children to a lonely and lost man.

Horace arrived at the four-story home with eight bathrooms, and seven bedrooms. He walked through the kitchen and saw the twelve hundred square foot wooden patio deck.

"Hey Jean, thanks for having me."
"No problem. We had to change plans. We're gonna eat inside. My back patio is getting' stained and sealed, so we're eating inside. Dawn's making a pork and potato stew. You're in the deck business, aren't ya? Anyway, Have a seat."

He sat down on a beautiful, comfortable, and fashionable new sofa. Jean seemed in an unusually giddy mood.

"Hey sport, you see this furniture . . . the sofa, the love seat . . . these end tables and ottomans . . . you see this stuff."
"Yeah, Jean, I see it. It's really nice stuff."
"I got a deal on it."
"Oh, really Jean. That's great."
"We knew this guy that needed to unload it, so we got a good deal on it."
"Great Jean. That's wonderful news."
"We paid $850 for the whole set. An inactive brother at our hall was dying of cancer and his worldly family had to get rid of it to help pay his medical bills."

69

Horace got up from his seat and ran into an empty pink room, the youngest daughter's room. She had her own bathroom. He ran into it and saw his reflection bright and large. It shocked him because he hadn't looked in a mirror in a month. It disgusted him. Then his eyes met the toilet sharply. He sat down. He felt inspired. He reached for a small, locked book, the little girl's diary. Horace broke the lock and used the small flowery pencil from inside. It didn't have an eraser, so he knew he had to get this right. The poem:

It's okay to be blind now
It's okay to be deaf

Having cleansed my soul
Having cleared all the blockage

I can sit in hollowed trees
I can see in caves of bats
I can look downward to the sky

It has left me.
I am free.

'Tis a colon I shall be . . .

He stood up.
He looked down to see a completely full toilet bowl.
He gently smiled (and why would he have smiled?).
He left the little girl's bathroom and shut the door behind him.

He didn't flush.

Part 3- Why did Denny Paint the Inside of the Doorknob Hole White? (Late 2006)

Denny took out the sandpaper, three grades of thickness. Was one of these correct for his job? It was, at the very least, a seventy-minute process to get more sandpaper.

Was this the correct sandpaper? He scrubbed the inside of the doorknob hole with a sponge. He easily compiled a list of supplies that reminded him of youthful days of light sunshine and the escape into his inground pool. Emotionally battered since, he read the list like fine wine in an elegant restaurant with a date who gazed lustfully into his eyes.

He laid down the materials on the screen door supported by two picnic table benches, painted and repainted dozens of times.

Paint brushes (three different sizes)
Paint (white)
Sandpaper
Bag of Weed
Chimney (pipe for marijuana)
Screwdriver
Hair Long, in his eyes
Skeleton Key

He gradually sipped a cup of water to prepare his throat to smoke weed from his chimney. He looked around. He stared. He sat silent. He picked up the thickest grade of sandpaper. Too thick, but the scientist in him decided to rub it against the inside of the doorknob hole anyway. He rubbed vigorously with veins and sweat popping from his temples. Behind his knee, a scent sprayed like from an unneutered cat looking for a mate. Flakes of wood and paint created a barnyard atmosphere in a 3 square inch part of the house directly underneath the doorknob hole.

Relationships were developed, consummated, and concluded in less time than it took for Denny to deem the first piece of sandpaper unusable. Onto the second piece but a voice in the distance interrupted him.

Horace came out of the backroom to begin breakfast.

Denny and Horace shared in cracking the shell of the egg after they spread the giant cast iron pan with butter. The wrinkled middle of their index fingers touched utilitarianly. Omega-3 breakfast fantasies charred their cholesterol passion while the last jalapeno from the urine yellow fridge, chopped square like individual Rubrik's Cube pieces, graced the corner of the plate. Horace and Denny cooked together regularly. It produced the highlight of their day. A day that usually started a tiny bit before 8pm and ended only a little after 8am.

Horace needed to take care of his wooden deck restoration business. Horace encouraged nighttime estimates and offered discounts to see a client's deck at 3am, instead of 3pm. He investigated the possibility of midnight crews for a cash discount.

Meanwhile, their eggs cackled with percussive power, which joined the loud Spanish conversation of the backyard neighbors. They owned a rooster out back. Denny noticed a tiny paint chip in the clear egg jism. Denny thought for a moment of how to get the eggshell splinter out, without disturbing the general shape and stature of the breakfast food.

"Shall I use a spatula or tweezers?" he whispered. "Shall I use my fingers or a fork?" He decided to use the long fingernail on the middle finger of his right hand and the thumbnail of his left hand. Magically, he formed a clamp and gently lowered his "Jaws of Life" fingernails into the pan. His thumbnail, an awkward shape, overlapped the length and width of his middle fingernail by about a tenth of an inch. The heat from the pan seared the three blond hairs that stuck out on his forefinger. A splotch of grease jumped just past his knuckle. When that occurred, Denny changed his mind and didn't pursue the eggshell. He thought about it later in the day. The incident replayed in his mind twelve or thirteen times. Each time the size of the eggshell grew; each time the grease burnt his knuckle to disfigurement and, eventually, to dismemberment. He fed that egg to Horace, and Horace didn't notice the shell.

Horace dreamt of Pat Beagley for the third time in the last decade. He remembered his last Pat Beagley dream with a vivid glow, when Pat created Michael and out he flew from her overstretched womb, mulatto in color, with a full-grown afro, stained with placenta juices and birth fluids. At twenty years old, she attended his Jehovah's Witness congregation in Cleveland. He, as an adolescent observer during the boredom of weekly meetings, noticed everything about her presence. Nobody knew of Pat's pregnancy because of her immense size and weight, but in Horace's repeated dream, he witnessed the birth, from the sex act with the father to be, to the flight of the infant into the hands of the stone-faced doctor. A Pat Beagley dream. A dream produced by the blurry Sunday and Friday night visions inside the sterile windowless confines of the Kingdom Hall.

Horace found a note in Denny's room. The note, simple and direct: Rachel's birthday, bring balloon. He forgot all about the note and glared at the hollow hole in the door. How long did Denny take with his sanding, his painting and waiting and repainting.

"Where's the metaphor in all of this?" he shouted as he threw a thin hair pick across the room. Each prong on the pick was a different color. The yellow prong broke off and bounced toward his feet. His bladder ached. His hands trembled. He reached for the screwdriver and walked out the door. He took a slight second to peer over his shoulder and back at the dark forest green house. It blended into its Theocratic Ministry B-School background like a green Braid sport coat during a discourse of disassociation. Horace remembered his leg shaking furiously and unconsciously. He'd squeeze his thigh until his thumbprints attached to his polyester heavyweight tough skins suit pants. The meetings still haunted him.

Horace could handle the ambiance of the local 1950s style hardware store. He saw a shining brass knob and chose it the way people choose a marriage mate. Horace, after he realized he cannot commit to a Jehovah's Witness sister, tried an online dating service once. He took an 80-question test that offered him the possibility to connect with his soulmate. When the service representative responded, the phone call and the subsequent explanation didn't go well.

The phone call:

Representative- "Hello Mr. Horace Brewer, it seems there was a little problem with your dating profile exam, particularly in the short answer section. We find your answers . . . well . . . let us say a bit uncomfortable. We don't know how to proceed."
Horace- "What's the problem?"
Representative- "Tell you what. We'll go ahead and send you an explanation with our profile expert's report."

Horace received his profile explanation in the mail.

Where do you see yourself in five years?

Answer- I see myself living in a cone shaped three-story dome and owning a windmill for energy.

How would you describe your outlook on life?

Answer- I realize that life is meaningless, but I try not to let it bother me too much.

Describe your favorite childhood memory:

Answer- We drove in my mother's red Chevy Chevette to the Kingdom Hall very early on Sunday morning. I sat in the back between Pat Beagley, Diane Synog, and Sister Zak.

Expert Profile Report:
We here at Find-your-Soulmate dating service feel that your answers are far too obscure and abstract to find you a match. Nobody answers D for number 73.

*   *   *

The concrete shed held the lawnmower, and something seemed to transport Horace to another intense Primosk memory. They met for a Saturday construction meeting, each of the Ministerial Servants that consisted of part-time fishermen, welders, carpenters, and landscapers to discuss the concrete shed designed to store the congregation lawnmower at the Kingdom Hall.

"Let's make it resemble an igloo or a short longhouse," the bricklayer suggested.

"Let's put a lock on the outside that requires an eighteenth-century skeleton key," the fisherman suggested.

Grandlin finally spoke up, "I can get a used lawnmower for $25 and fix it up."

Everyone agreed on an igloo shaped concrete shed. "It's blizzard proof," they all said in unison.

Later, Horace quickly filled the hole with the knob. When Denny noticed, he grinned.

*   *   *

Diane Synog joined The Watchtower during the Rutherford era. She raised her only daughter in the religion. Her only daughter, Rachel, grew up attending the Kingdom Hall in Cleveland, but when her single mother became inactive, Rachel, age 13, stopped attending, as well. Sometimes Rachel roller-skated to disco lights on LSD. She read books alone in the school cafeteria, things like *Civilization and its Discontents*, *The Complete Works of Edgar Allen Poe*, and *Orlando* by Virginia Woolfe. Now, some ten years later, she sat at the hospital bed to watch her anointed grandmother die.

She looked forward to her birthday, and she wondered if Denny would remember and be on time with the balloon. Her fate depended on a man that took three years to produce and edit a wedding video. By the time Denny finished the video, the married couple already divorced and hated one another. Denny didn't realize this fact and sent the DVD recording with this note (Rachel pictured Denny reading it):

Hello there, Rico. Sorry it took so long to get this video to you. Have a happy marriage. May you stay together for years and years untold. May your children bear fruit like an organic raspberry bush.

Meanwhile, Diane Synog slowly faded to death. Synog died at 96 and lived from Russell's death to the first print of the purple song book to the overlapping generation belief, and she made her last words resound loud and clear to her granddaughter. "Rachel, I'm dying. You know that. I've lived a good life. A full life thanks to you and the rest of the family. A rainbow

I'll send for you to enjoy one week from today. I am going to heaven. I realize you are a unbeliever and have been influenced by the existential-atheist crowd. I know you feel nausea when you have to be in large groups of ordinary people. Promise me one thing Rachel. Promise me you'll find hope and faith in the one true religion. Jehovah exists." And with those words, Synog signed off.

*   *   *

Horace ran from the slightly dilapidated lakeside home with his miner's light on his head. He greeted Denny with a mighty handshake, and they walked down to Richard Termer's house. The house sat in the woods, near a lake, not on a lake like Horace told Denny, and when Denny noticed them walking farther and farther away from the lake, he remained emotionless. He felt exactly the same. He didn't care if the house was on a lake.

Horace introduced him to his shirtless accountant, Richard Termer. Denny accepted Termer's polar bear persona and thought to himself, "Well, I'll be damned. Horace was right. This guy does look kind of like a polar bear, but kind of like a fast food postmodern twenty-first century mutation of a post-greenhouse effect polar bear."

Denny sat emotionless. The night moved along as Termer stared into his toaster oven which held a fifty-dollar steak hostage.

Termer stared with the intensity of a bullfighter into the small greased stained appliance. His brain processed each second the meat cooked. He noticed a new line in the steak and tiny increases in fluid that rested atop the steak. When something dramatic happened like fat popping or grease spilling, he concentrated more. His biological clock alerted him when the steak was done. It all came natural to Termer.

77

Denny approached Termer meekly and delicately asked, "How do you like your steak?" Termer stumbled a little as the question disrupted his concentration. For Termer there were no quantum leaps, he thought of everything, every motion. He processed every word. "I . . . ahhh . . . I . . . like it well done."

"Where are you from Termer?"

"West Virginia City, Virginia."

Denny asked no further questions but did offer to smoke a joint with him. Termer accepted the offer.

Horace, afraid of being disfellowshipped, did not smoke, but watched the relationship between the two worldly men with keen attention and affection. Horace's mouth opened as a crescent moon appears on a dark mountain night. At times he'd cross his arms elbow to elbow. At other times he laughed with a gentle boyish innocence. Horace embraced these special moments. Two worldly strangers becoming quick friends. He understood the difficulties of making a trustworthy friend while inside The Watchtower and how it seemed so much more natural on the outside. Termer and Denny. Denny and Termer. They smoked and smoked more pot.

Termer continued to hold the joint, taking as many as three hits at a time, defying pot smoking etiquette. He apologized by stating that he was letting it cool off. Denny's glare fixated on the cigarette. He wanted to hold it really bad. Denny never heard of the concept of a joint cooling off.

Horace perceived a competition develop between the two men. He said to himself, "There's a contest, and the winner is the guy who takes the last hit off the joint."

Termer sucked and sucked on the joint and forget about his now overcooked steak. Denny took a hit, never breaking the code. Termer took three hits and passed it back. The joint had become a roach. Its edges seared like an old pirate's treasure map as the contest grew more and more serious. Termer's thick fingers made it tough to hold, and he showed some signs of giving up. His wobbled a little, and Horace noticed him teeter a bit to a scoliosis posture. His invisible trapeze act did not shake Denny who possessed much smaller fingers. Fingers more suited to grasp a third of an inch piece of fiery rolling paper. Horace watched, mesmerized by the minuteness of the roach, smaller and smaller it got, after lighting and relighting. Soon both men desperately attempted to relight it. It ended in a tie. Neither took a last hit and gained a but a mutual respect for one another.

Termer devoured his burnt steak while Horace pictured a final soy hot dog on a grill.

"So Termer, do you exercise much?" Denny questioned.
"I just joined a gym," Termer responded with a black char in his smile, "Virginia City Fitness." They both laughed hysterically and hugged.

*   *   *

The stench of the apple cider vinegar lingered like the excrement of a giant Mayan bat in a lost pyramid cave. Denny didn't notice. To keep his meter stick length hair healthy, he decided to stop using "shampoo chemicals." His excursions to the bathroom for his cleaning sometimes lasted hours.

Over a short period of time, Horace grew curious of Denny's marathon bathroom visits and set up a tiny digital camera in the light fixture to spy. Obviously, he did not want to be caught, but he took the risk and set up the homemade wire contraption.

Denny took out a set of nail clippers and four q-tips. The puffy end of one q-tip receded to the point where a tiny portion of the reinforced paper stick revealed itself. He noticed this and attempted to reshape the thinning cotton. He wondered if a tiny piece of scotch tape might help. He thought, "I wouldn't want the glue from the tape to melt in my ear." He put the q-tip aside and thought about what to do next. Meanwhile, he took out a pair of scissors and started to trim the micro hairs on the edge of his ear lobe. He stopped and stared at the scissors. Horace, excited with anticipation, leaned forward in his chair as he studied each movement.

Denny continued to stare at the scissors. The scissors looked back at Denny. He reached into a small leather case for a Phillips screwdriver and delicately fit it into the screw at the center of the scissors. He turned his wrist and fingers. It proved too big for the screw. Screwdriver number two stood mysterious in the back of the case. This dirty and gritty screwdriver fit. Denny tightened the screw. Witnessing all of this, Horace nearly fell off his couch.

Denny scratched his knee. He specifically used the nail of his middle finger because it had a crack that provided a very sharp blade. Horace looked at his own middle finger. Denny vanished out of view into some unknown corner of the bathroom. Horace screamed, "NO!" He spilled his popcorn onto the floor and one of the cats ate a kernel. "Where are you?" Then, he bent forward and yelled, "What are you doing?" Denny reappeared, and Horace fell back to his chair relaxed and relieved. He whispered, "Thank Jehovah," without realizing that Termer sat in the next room. Termer heard and asked, "Thank Jehovah? For what, Horace?" Before Horace answered, Termer noticed the screen that pictured Denny in the bathroom. They both watched like delirious monkeys with a sense of unconscious purpose.

Denny's elbow bent; his chin wrinkled; his eye blinked; his hand tightened; his throat swallowed. He rubbed his eye. The random movements froze Termer and Horace. To them it was like watching the construction of a pyramid or a rare Navajo performance of a sun dance. It was a lunar eclipse and a mystic tree root. He showered now, faithfully grabbing the leafy organic soap, rubbing it against his hands and almost creating a fire from the friction and the foliage. Lather never developed. He could not produce suds or gentle bubbles for his pale skin. He rubbed harder and scraped his palm until it was brush burnt. Two droplets of blood lay on his skin and remained. Even with all the water falling on him from the brass showerhead, they remained. He noticed the blood and sucked it up as if it were swamp algae from the Precambrian period. His underarm hair resembled curled wire mesh like a knight's chainmail. He held his razor in hand like a sword. They could see his thoughts as he shaved. "First, I will remove the hair from just under my chin. It is the most brittle, almost bonelike. Then I will add a touch more cod liver oil and vitamin E powder to my mustache. There that's it, just enough. Don't squeeze too much or else . . . more hot water. I wish this sink were an eighth of an inch deeper directly in the center, that way I could rest the razor at a perfect 17-degree angle, while *I* rest. My toothbrush needs to be soaked in whey eagle extract. I bought some off the Internet, and it may work. Where's that floss, did Horace leave it in his room?"

Horace looked on, mesmerized by the enchanting routine. Termer got up to get some pork rinds and fell asleep standing up. Denny's skin never wrinkled, not for a second. Somehow, he figured out a way to saturate his body in warm water for hours without shriveling. His mucilage-colored toothpaste poured out of the jar at the same rate as Denny lived life. They joined together in life rhythm.

"Holy Melaleuca!" Horace exclaimed.

*   *   *

"There are things happening around you that you don't understand," screamed Rachel into her mirror. She usually thought deeply in frequent existential stupors. That morning she spotted a fig tree in the sidewalk standing with the posture of an arthritic giraffe. She called Denny every day for the past two weeks with no reply. She left spontaneous messages. Every time she left a message, she realized that she should have prepared something to say. It didn't matter much because Denny never heard a single message. He didn't have his own phone or voicemail. He couldn't be texted. Anyone who wanted to communicate with Denny had to call one of Horace's many phone numbers. Horace never answered the phone either. Horace just might relay a message Denny, but usually not. So, the messages Rachel left existed on an assortment of different voicemails at the mercy of Horace's concept time and space. The last real correspondence she shared with Denny was a note she quickly passed to him on a rainy morning in a Cleveland homeless shelter. It read, "Rachel's birthday, bring balloon." She wondered if Denny remembered.

*   *   *

Denny, meanwhile, plucked a stray hair from his pointy left shoulder. The hair didn't fit in with the rest on his body. It confused him every time he showered. He felt powerless at the sight of it. "That buzzard just keeps growing back. Doesn't it?"

*   *   *

Rachel entered her grandmother's basement. The mold conquered her scent glands. The hundred-year-old wine press rusted its bolts for permanent hibernation. Upon seeing her reflection in an antique mirror, she peered at her dark hair and dark eyes. She smiled. She sensed all of it down there, all the old Cleveland industries and pastimes. The decaying Lake Erie fish left over from Bethlehem Steel pollution; the

82

union strikes; the boating middle class; Brian Sipe; rust belt decay; bridges and innocent bystanders.

Otis Synog, her grandfather, burst though the guardrail during the great white death blizzard in 1977. His ice fishing turned into a disaster, so Rachel never knew him. She wasn't told about his car falling ninety feet off the top of the bridge.

Rachel was born one year later, on the exact day of the blizzard, and now, in her grandmother's empty abandoned house, she could feel him. The poem he wrote survived the crash. It sat under a stack of his other poems.

Rachel read the first:

Harvest my ego with time's distant
companion
At odds with separation's anxiety
I reach to slide off her glasses imagining
the kiss to follow
we are gentle together
we are lambs mid-day spring's bubbling and
taste as pure as Jehovah's tears.

Out of the side of her eye she saw her grandmother in a black and white pose of youth. Nineteen forties maybe nineteen thirties and elegant. Rachel lit some incense that she always carried. She read another poem:

Snowy street of urban night café
winds cool desolate wine
drum beat
shared hand glove
saxophone entrance
brandy
legs in unison
walk

knee to thigh
thigh to knee
connected
crystal ring

She read on:

At the center of the frozen lake
Which I see in the distance
Atop this giant bridge
You are there, and I will be frozen in it
Please tell me you are in the center waiting
Please provide a gentle hug as I die
from car's collapse
The day moon is your eye that sees me fall
To my death

Rachel froze. She felt the chill of the lake. She could feel the explosion of steel and rubber. She could hear him scream as his car hung in the sky. Waiting, as Jehovah held it, suspended.

"Love," Rachel whispered to herself.

Conflict erupted in her heart as she remembered her grandmother's upcoming funeral.

*   *   *

Denny used a ten-inch piece of pinecone floss and took a toothpick from his rolling toothpick dispenser. He owned two different dispenser models. One he bought at the last garage sale on his street before the toxic waste under its foundation caused it to close. A restless carpenter who owned several types of salt-water fish in an aquarium that lived in his living room constructed the other one. Denny remembered the dazzling variety of colors of his aquatic life, and he also remembered how quickly they all died, the more beautiful, the shorter their lives. He saw the fluorescent orange fish decay at the bottom on the glittering rocks. He witnessed the neon green swimmers melt and float as a gooey nuclear substance.

Horace shut off his screen and let Denny finish without an audience. Termer fell asleep and woke up several more times and finally found himself sleeping in the sink under the faucet with water flowing up his nose.

By now it was 11pm, and Denny stepped out of the bathroom. Near his big toe hung some lint. Denny used some wire pipe cleaners as toe floss. Horace saw and screamed, "Are you using a caterpillar to get rid of that toe lint?"

Horace lived only two miles from Denny when he made the phone call that started their relationship.

*   *   *

Rachel sat on the plastic covered bed. "Otis the poet, my granddad, Otis a poet." She sat and thought:

Daylight decides visions divine . . . Daylight decides visions divine . . . DAYLIGHT DECIDES VISIONS DIVINE . . . she screamed, "DAYLIGHT DECIDES VISIONS DIVINE!"

*   *   *

Horace spoke to Mr. Wister, Denny's father. "Hi sir. Is Denny available?" Horace waited calmly for a response.

"He's in his subterranean hovel sleeping. He had twelve phone calls, 46 emails, and his air mattress has deflated. The only thing between him and the floor is a centimeter of soft camping rubber."

Mr. Wister provided this descriptive answer with his monotone accountant wit. His words lay like numbers in columns. Dry dead words deteriorated by the social bacteria of life. Horace, eager to speak to his mysterious new friend, urged the man to wake up his sleeping son. "Please, Mr. Wister. I really must speak to him."

Suddenly he heard, "Good Morning!"
"Hey, this is one of Taze's friends, and he suggested that I contact you about some legal work in Virginia."

Denny hadn't peed for twenty-six hours:

His bladder the great canopy of Noah
Sacrifice under the rainbow
Toil for soil

Denny needed to pee passionately, but Horace kept talking.

"Did Taze say anything about me? I'm about 2 miles away. Can I come and see you?"
"Give me an hour." Denny took a "garlinger" pee into an empty aluminum can of diet peach Arizona Iced Tea and fell back asleep.

*   *   *

Horace looked at a sleeping, hollow, and brittle Denny. Denny escaped the sun's rays, and his face could not flush anymore. His toes twitched, pinky to big toe with a precise rhythm, each time. Horace kept track with his watch.

three seconds
twitch
three seconds
twitch
three seconds
twitch

Denny's life beat. This mirrors his speed and initiative. Horace noticed the jaw line bulging and tight, top and bottom fighting for space. Cavity against cavity, wisdom against wisdom. Then they made a scraping noise, and Denny's mouth moved. Horace tapped Denny's foot and turned around.

"Hand me that pipe," the command casually fell from Denny's mouth.
Horace turned back to see a face smiling and sitting up. "This pipe?" Horace questioned.
"That's the one." Horace picked it up. He couldn't help but examine the pipe. "Do you want to smoke?" Denny asked.

Diane Synog's Funeral

Rachel interpreted the grotesque sterility of the funeral home as another symbol for God's death. She entered grateful of the fact that her grandfather put beauty into the world. They asked her to speak:

"I discovered beauty this afternoon in the form of words. Watching my grandmother die reinforced the ugliness of existence."

The attendees could feel Rachel's nervousness and her confusion. Rachel began to lick her top lip.

"But her dying sentiment was a request, not just for me, but for every one of us . . . everyone on the earth. She said to believe in Jehovah. My answer is how can any human believe in Jehovah when all we see is suffering, pollution, pain, rejection, disloyalty." Her voice cracked like a tuba note, "dishonesty, stupidity, and . . . and . . . and . . . a real lack of beauty. All of us must become like Otis, my grandfather, who now resides with grandma in the stormy waters of Lake Erie. He was an artist. There *is* a place for the artist in this world."
People became very uncomfortable.

"We must write poems and make films. We must compose symphonies and paint pictures. WE MUST

87

DESTROY THOSE THAT DESTORY ART!'"
Rachel lost all dignity and passed out.

Denny's Basement

Ten months earlier in Denny's basement, Horace
refused a hit from Denny's pipe because after
examination, it looked like an eleventh century
monastery chimney.

*   *   *

The swirling water served as a magnet to Denny's
eyes. His head looped around as the typhoon disposed
of his triangle urine. He opened the medicine chest
with the mirror clear and indifferent. His shadow hung
on the ceiling and glared into the thinning spot atop
Denny's head. He washed his hands. Following that,
he scratched his foot in a spot where three weed like
hairs sprung up. He then gave his own shoulder a
quick athletic rub down.

He went to clean out the litter boxes. Shaking the
small vacuum cleaner, he noticed that the bag for
collecting filth needed to be changed, but he knew that
he didn't have any bags left. "Ahh . . . should I wait
and do this later after I get the vacuum bags, or
should I try to clean the litter pans with the
appliance?"

Denny heard the voice of Mr. Wister, his father,
"Denny are you changing the litter? If you are, we
don't have any extra vacuum bags, so don't do it."
"I noticed that dad, what should we do?"
"Well . . . we can either wait on cleaning the litter, or
we can try cleaning it without the vacuum. Son of a
bitch, I was just shopping at Schictal's, too."
"Yeah, well . . . what should I do?"
Horace sat in the basement and waited and observed
the odd surroundings. Everything seemed organized
into small compartments, and when Horace opened
one up, he found an even smaller compartment inside.

Eventually, the compartments disappeared. Nothing left inside, just some dust and air, just a sprinkling of powder that dissolved instantly. Two giant computers dominated the corner with speakers, cameras, and instruments. Wires and more wires formed an Ivy League football stadium, switches and knobs written in Japanese, pedals, levers, buttons, clips, and nails hung from the wall. Dartboards caked with toxic residue, bows and arrows of Boy Scout youth. Train sets that paralleled the fate of the actual railway. Coal miners trapped. G.I. Joe's decimated. Emphysema floated in the air.

*   *   *

Denny returned, and they talked of glue sticks and tree branches. They spoke of trails in the desert sand and musicians who swayed their heads to bongos and congas. They dreamt of nutmeg peanut butter on wheat toast with the hashish giraffe on New Year's.

"Tell me about you and Taze together. You know, as friends."

"I guess there's not much to say. We tried LSD together back in summer 1997 and plugged in the guitar."

"What happened?"

"Taze kept playing the same note over and over again with . . . I think it was a D note. He played it with a vibrato pedal."

"How did it sound?"

"I don't know. I was watching the ceiling fan spin. Anyway, he kept playing this note over and over again for twenty minutes. In the meantime, my parents came home."

"Mr. Wister?"

"Yes. I'm not sure how long he listened to the noise, but eventually he said, 'Denny, what the fuck is going on down here?'"

Horace laughed.

Horace could see Denny's history, one of merit badges, microscopes, military planes, wood paneling, bleached sidewalk misery, café addendums, self-hating. They talked:

"What do you know about Taze?"
"He's been my friend for a while now. He blinks a lot. He's nervous. You could always see it from a distance, a man blinking, a man defenseless in silence. I saw him fall from the top of a slide in the desert, dust filled his pant legs, and he mangled his toes. He didn't realize the impact of the sun parch rust spots of the 1975 car roof slide. The angular issues of scratched kneecaps and unbuttoned buttons and instantaneous fraternal blood seemed to fill his consciousness." Denny paused after the rant. He felt embarrassed because of his creative and healthy description of Taze.

Horace started to interrupt, but Denny began again, "He helped us with the pool cover last summer. He injured his back for a couple days. The chlorine residue burned tart into his pallet, his taste buds . . . I mean. I remember that his parents never fixed the wooden fence or killed the algae in the pool."

Horace stood fascinated, not by Denny's words alone, but by them and the odd addition of his giraffe like posture (an aesthetic sight of radical godly art.)

*   *   *

In 1978, the year Emory grew his sideburns a half an inch longer and a quarter and a third centimeter deeper, these people united in marriage. Diane Synog Jr. (Rachel's mother) designed the floral arrangements for their future divorce. It is here where a three-year-old Horace met Rachel who was one month from being born and full of womb activity. Horace felt a strange connection to the movements of her and, somehow, sensed her communication with him. He sensed her fear at the prospect of leaving her mother and entering the cold harsh realities of Cleveland life. From what she could perceive, it didn't seem as safe and pleasant as her present existence.

She knew her father lost his factory job and took to having whisky dinners in snow's reflective glare. She felt the cold and ice.

Just one sound encouraged her to consider her birth. Diane walked away to fix a flower that she accidentally knocked over on her way to shake Darnell's hand. A slew of random events blocked Horace's view of Diane. Primosk laughed at a Panzerelle joke; Brots adjusted his tiepin, and Dombrowsky sat alone sighing.

When he finally got sight of Diane, he walked over with "strimple" curiosity and listened again to Rachel's thoughts. "When are we going home, mom?" "Why is it so loud?" Horace tried to communicate with her using his mind.

"Rachel, Rachel, why are we here?"

Nothing back.

Horace thought harder and harder, "Rachel, Rachel." "What!" She yelled. Horace took a step back and put one finger in his left ear.
"It's Horace."
"Horace? Who is Horace?"
"I am"
"I'm Rachel."
"I know. It seems like you're about to be born any day now. Does that make you happy?"
"No. I'm disgusted by the lifestyle of my parents. They watch disco ball dancing on TV and play with fondue sticks and have friends that smoke green and black ceremonial tobacco."
"Yeah, that's sounds about right. Do you know anything about the factories closing their doors?"

91

"My father lost his job. I know that. Making a living is awful. Are there any redeeming factors in life outside the womb?"

He thought, using a different part of his brain, so that Rachel couldn't hear. He answered, "No."
Rachel was surprised. "There is one thing that seems to make it worth doing," she stated firmly.
"What is that?"
"Well, it's not a possession, and it isn't really tangible like a gift, but it is something that people can share."

He had no idea what she was getting at.

"Horace, there's a story my grandmother always repeats to my mother about the feelings her and my grandfather had for each other."
"What is this feeling?" Horace grew impatient.
"I guess it's love. That's the reason."
Diane walked away.

* * *

Denny drove late in the night without his license or registration, which he literally didn't have because of his personal abstract rebellion.

The back of the car filled quickly with an array of objects: receipts, twine, clothespins, guitar strings, Arby's uniform, organic oranges. He drove on and on through hills and trees that appeared as blackness to him.

Filling up on gas, chips, and an egg salad sandwich. His gut in anguish. He never drank coffee but chose the short nap technique on long drives. Most fifteen-minute naps existed only in theory or in the laboratory but not at three am in northern Virginia. Many gas stations didn't accept gold for payment. Rarely did Denny have cash, and never credit, only gold, which "gained in value everyday while cash dropped."

He dreamt of the animal farm windmill as his cone shaped erect tower. His hair dangled like a lost nursery rhyme. He dreamt of Rachel and the note she crunched into his hand so desperately. She continued to try to get him to embrace existential thought, quoting Sartre and Wise King Solomon. She declared repeatedly, "Life is meaningless." He found this difficult to deal with because of his involvement in economic and legal activism. One night he read from the Black's law dictionary and also a romance novel. In the morning, he imagined a torrid affair followed by mundane divorce court proceedings.

He screamed into the dismal 3:23 am sky and shouted, "Why do I have these obligations to these people? Why must I be responsible to communicate rationally within the current framework of socio-artistic organization?"

He felt as though everyone crowded around him like red ants in the jungle. He felt like the last man.

*   *   *

Her funeral treatise left her unconscious. She chased an unidentified pedestrian into the eternity of her unconsciousness.

She chased him into a corner. She screamed in his face. Her anger uncontrollable and her deep harsh words piercing his ego.

"Say something unique! I will read something to you. Listen up!" Her voice sounded like a vibrato organ gasp:

And now good-morrow to our waking souls,
Which watch not one another out of fear

For love all love of other sights controls
And makes one little room an everywhere.

She read in a profoundly sad tone. "What does that
mean?" She screamed. "What does it mean to you?
Tell me!" She completely cornered the man. He
couldn't go anywhere, forced to listen to Rachel.
"What does it mean to you?" On the verge of violence,
Rachel almost lost control.

"I don't know," The man replied.
"Listen to me!"

And now good-morrow to our waking souls,
Which watch not one another out of fear
For love all love of other sights controls
And makes one little room an everywhere.

"Think about it. Listen and think."
"But I don't know what it means. I am sorry."
"Change your life then! Change!"
She continued, "Just one thought please . . . just one
creative thought from your mouth."

And now good-morrow to our waking souls
Which watch not one another out of fear
For love all love of other sights controls And
makes one little room an everywhere.

What does it mean to you?"
                    *   *   *
Horace wished she would say those magic words. He
stared into the face of a woman who couldn't
understand Jehovah's Witness life. He wanted her to
acknowledge the natural vibrations that emanated
from a table that folded from a wall in the most
auspicious of places, next to the Watchtower bound
volumes: 1881-1912.

Will she remember and tell him all about how Brother Brade was sent by the Presiding Overseer to select the correct size urinal and came back with one his own Indian height?

Horace wanted more than anything to hear those words, to see the formation of the lips and the rise of the tongue as she articulated the term "Let us dismiss for the B-SCHOOL!"

Horace would never hear those words. It didn't matter how many women he brought back to see Termer's cassette player and toaster oven.

Horace sat on the couch with one woman, and Termer walked out of his bedroom. He didn't notice Horace and the woman. Termer laid his giant ape gut onto the pretend wood grain countertop. It sat perfectly between his two knives and three plastic gas station cups. Horace remembered how he got up every morning to the sound of pseudo-jazz and watched Termer dance a homemade variation of the peppermint twist which resembled Godzilla on an OxyContin rush. Termer poured enormous cups of coffee. His bacon grease, slow moving, backed up in his colon.

Denny used his finger to wipe a slight blueberry preserve stain from the pair of jeans he hadn't taken off in forty-seven hours.

Horace, Denny, and Termer: Their expectations diminished greatly over time. Could this trinity of demoralized men thrive? Denny's consciousness erupted with this thought as he noticed a grain of black pepper on the albino arm of Termer. He discovered, without even asking, that one time, a long time ago, Termer wanted to be a pro football tackle or guard. He coveted the Forest Gregg award and threw horseshoes to practice his long snap. Sometimes at picnics he'd played lawn darts.

Horace dreamt about the garage skis, moving trucks and the used Mercedes always in the driveway. Whose coleslaw was the best? They both used the precious and sought after Smoke's Creek water, a spring, which provided virtually pure water. One could simply put a cup in the water and drink. Only one case of beaver fever ever recorded: 1975.

On the couch of semen's splendor, Horace read his Edgar Allen Poe when he could. He especially enjoyed the perverted buried alive story. He'd look intensely at the picture of the colon on the wheat germ cleanser jar. Termer usually responded well to TV advertisements. His consumerism for most goods ended in the late 1980's cassette killing vinyl era, but when it came to video games, he was up to date. He didn't realize it played audio CDs, as well, so when Denny asked him if he could play some psychedelic music, Termer reflected a moment and said, "I don't have a cd player." Instead of pushing the issue, Denny relented deciding not to embarrass Termer by exposing his ignorance of his own purchased and much used technology. Denny wondered to himself with disappointment and Buddhist confusion, "How could this man spend twelve or thirteen hours a day using this machine and not realize it plays CDs?" "Doesn't the game look just like a CD?"

Horace flicked a pot seed across the room and flashbacked to jury duty 1997 and his wild discovery of Schitel embezzlement at TV shop. To his surprise, the man he knew to pull all the deals, hand out the pens and velemints, sold uhf antennae in the black market. Although the technology would be obsolete by the time the suit was brought against him, his actions in the dim Watchtower apocalyptic early 1980's came back upon him like a boomerang. This lawsuit, for less than $3000, ran through small claims court, and Horace made the sneaky and mischievous mistake of pretending he didn't recognize the name James Schictel alias "The Sheik." When it came time for trial, Horace sat in disguise with fake beard and bleached eyebrows turning his head uncomfortably trying to avoid being seen by the hand cuffed Schictel.

Horace's bushy hair stood up straight as he dozed off and spilled some wine on the carpet. The wine stained the floor immediately. He rolled off the couch saturating his elbow in it.

It seemed like a purposeless day until Denny stormed into the room. He held up a cleaned paintbrush. Horace knew Denny stood at the sink for an hour or so and thought, "Something in this house is being worked on. Something is being fixed or cleaned or cleared up or tuned up. Some sort of obscure and almost irrelevant act of civilized living is being performed by Denny."

It must have involved a tool, water, and manpower. Denny finished the painting of all the insides of the doorknobs. He put away all the utensils and instruments required for the job. The brushes were cleaned; the sandpaper recycled; the butter knife polished; the lighter stored in the ever-shrinking weed sack; the fingernails trimmed and straightened; the wood chips swept up; he even blew his nose. He was cleansed, cleaned, wholly repaired and had nothing to worry about. All of the work attached to the doorknob holes completed. Everything. No more towels or knee pads or rubbing or scratching. No more thoughts of what to do and what order to do it in. His struggle of deciding whether to put the screwdriver or the sandpaper away first dissipated and dissolved. The decisions were made. Horace was proud of Denny, but when Denny noticed the small wine stain on Termer's carpet, peace was destroyed, and a thousand overwhelming thoughts of its eventual disappearance hit Denny's mind.

Horace slipped further and further into a near comatose flashback. He thought of all the names in his past. His brain automatically organized them into graphs, charts, games and puzzles. His brain went like this:

He created a crossword puzzle with no effort. It flowed from his soul.

Across
5. Dated, got baptized
7. Eldest son of Keith
10. Circuit overseer with pompadour
11. Formerly named Keith changed name to Gary
13. Fisherman
14. Overweight teen grandson
15. Anointed

Down
1. Infant son who refused blood transfusion
2. Former owner of A-Z
3. Polish biological sisters
4. Grumpy man, handed out candy
5. Disfellowshipped in '82 reinstated '90
8. Prayed over bread at '83 memorial
12. Event where one sees all Bugala kids

He constructed word problems:

The book study is at Schictal's house and starts at 7:30pm. If Termer is heading south on East and West Road at 37 mph at 7:27pm, will he arrive on time if Schictal's house is one and half miles away?

Sometimes he'd just make statements of fact:

1.Kirby Crooms lent his trumpet to Yohannas.
2.She wore a 40 DD brazier on Dona.
3.Fugate was an amateur plumber.
4.He had a very shiny waxed ass after hockey.

Denny didn't know these people and, when Horace tried to explain the significance of elaborate Schictel family day pre-door-to-door lunches with shanks of baloney and giant mustard jars, Denny didn't understand. He couldn't comprehend the overweight polish people over 60 years old.

*   *   *

1 Denny is not a simpleton and should not be interpreted as such. He seals his screwdrivers in zip lock security. He does not get angry unless with cats. Guard yourself against the belief that Denny lacks the complexities of a modern man.

2 There are deceivers out there "roaming about like wicked lions" and they are "ready to deceive" in this Termer of the End. In the book of Horacen, we read of how a prophet from Ridge Road will "rise up out of Smoke's Creek" and lead a rebellion against timely solutions and repairs. We know that it is wrong to use our time unwisely by participating in activities that are "efficient and speedy." Today in our study, we will read the first seven verses of Horacen chapter three and apply this prophecy to our modern day.

3 Horacen 3:1-3: "I heard a loud voice in the distance, 'Out from Bogardas and legs of Earl three stars are seen through clouds of past rain. Each one will carry its member to the Isle of Grand, and they will see a man with sass and glowing fish. And as they walk, Smoke's Creek will fill and from it will rise a wise man of slow duty and no reliability. He will teach the slow ones to disintegrate, and he will teach the fast ones to be slow ones and all society will be altered.' This is the voice I heard."

4 From these verses, we note the characteristics and location of the great prophet of procrastination and sloth motivation. The main identifying mark of this prophet would be the length of time it takes for him to complete a routine task. As of yet, we do not know what the task is, but it will certainly be recognized by those "who see visions of apathetic grandeur." (Bus 1:7) In this Termer of the End, it is our goal and focus to listen and respond to all of the counsel presented by this class of people. No one else on earth can decipher the meaning and relevance to Denny and the prophecy in Horacen.

5Everyday new ones are coming to appreciate the material that is presented by the visionaries. Let us consider the next verse at Horacen 3:4, "And when he rises it will take him many hours, nay, years to complete the chopping of the mere sapling bush. And the bush will burn with the flames of solemn laziness, and the appetite of the wise men will be felled in the forest from the single ax cut of the prophet. Preparing the ax for chopping will be an eternity to times indefinite. He will use the oil from the pigeon bowel, the flint from the sea coral, and the semen of the last land lizard. All will be turned on its side. And there is a moment of relaxation as he smokes the sacred herb of Fugate."

6In this Termer of the End, we are starving for the rise of this prophet, and he will provide for us from nature. Even though it may take centuries for him to close his sandal, the wait will be well worth it when we have no more fear of being late or being too busy to sit on a couch or look at a computer screen. All else can be pushed aside in favor of passive activities. No more need will we have for hurrying or scuttling like land crabs toward the ocean of time limits.

1. (a)What should Denny not be interpreted as? (b) Where will Denny rise up from and

how?

2, 3. What prophecy is presented in chapter 3 in the book of Horacen, and how does it affect us today?

4.In this Termer of the End, what will the prophet do in the forest?

5.Discuss the pigeon bowel.

6.(a) What are we starving for in this Termer of the End? (b) What do we no longer have to fear? (c) What will we have no need for?

*   *   *

Horace shivered on the plaid distorted couch. He texted while the television played old wedding videos. He had pieced together the highlights of each of his friend's weddings into one long perfect wedding where the dresses flowed, the speeches moved, the dances stirred, the cakes smeared, the kisses wooed, the vows sang, the reception halls glittered, the guests toasted, and the food melted on the tongue. Horace wanted a marriage to a Watchtower woman but found it almost impossible to find a PIMO one. On top of being PIMO, he wanted her to be able to converse about a broad range of academic topics like history, philosophy, literature, music, and wholistic medicine. It proved exhausting to try to read through the lines of a Watchtower woman's speech. Even if he suspected a Watchtower woman of being PIMO, he had no idea how to ask. One time he took the chance:

"Are you PIMO," he asked meekly.

"Emo?"

"No. No. PIMO."

"What's that?"

"It means Physically In Mentally Out."

"Out of what?"

"Out of the Truth. The Watchtower."

"No. Why are you asking me this? Are you ahhh..."

"PIMO."

"Yeah, whatever . . . are you PIMO?"

"No. Um. No."

"Then, why did you ask me?"

"Because you . . . well, because you don't go to all the meetings. You wear . . . you know . . . worldly clothes."

"You sound like my dad."

* * *

Horace called out to Termer. Did he forget that Termer died? Or was it some sort of Freudian slip seeping out of his gaping grit paste mouth? Denny's open mouth and trumpeted horrible deadly sounds of corpse snoring. He had collapsed and fell asleep instantly.

Horace stepped on his head without knowing so. "Termer? Termer?"

"He's dead," Denny said.

Horace walked away unmoved and thought, "Denny always speaks in metaphors,"

Denny realized that Horace didn't understand that Termer actually died earlier by suicide. With a stare, Denny conveyed the message. Horace and Denny quickly embraced and shed tears of meek irrelevance. A voice interrupted them.

"Who is that? Is that Termer?" asked Horace.

"No, he's dead. It must be the Ghost of Termer!" exclaimed Denny.

Termer said, "Remember Rachel's birthday. Remember the balloon."

Denny felt faint. He had to complete two major obligations in very limited time. Then, Termer's ghost disappeared in a mist that smelled vaguely of back sweat.

Denny sat and stared into the muted reflection returning from the TV set. He realized that the ghost of Termer surpassed Casper by at least a ton.

* * *

102

Cleveland did not get the best of him yet. Horace could still contentedly walk with bare feet that touched the blades of weeds that seeped through the cracked sidewalks and pavement of the dreary lake front park. The lake no longer served as a means for the health of the people anymore. Industrial waste filled the space. A pure dumping ground for thick chemical substances. A combination of fresh water and synthetic manufacturing ingredients. The guardrails dangled and only the excessive rust of the hardware held them together. The frames of buildings miraculously hung without foundations in the air with the exception of an occasional moment where gravity worked.

"In this place, even gravity is dead," Horace thought. "Life has no meaning!" He shouted, "Life is a series of abstract random actions incapable of being understood by empirical and emotional intuitiveness alone. Something else must know, something not made in the image of man."

Rachel walked the streets along the river, too, and their ghosts agreed to meet in this dream. She whistled and panted heavy because she just quit smoking. She'd rationalize continuously to her grandmother that the "air pollution in Cleveland is worse than cigarette smoke." This dream occurred with the old Rachel, the one any existentialist could call for reassurance that God is still dead. She lived with constant nausea and, occasionally, at the time, practiced the dialect of a Buddhist for political purposes or for a possible date. Existentialist men proved difficult to find, especially the ones with jobs or good post graduate grades. She contacted a dating service and received a short questionnaire.

1. What are your ultimate goals in life, financially speaking?

103

I refuse to sell my labor or involve myself in any Christmas celebrations, even if my mate's family requires it . . . even if I break all of the artificial moral codes of an entire village. The mad man comes down the hill!

2. What age bracket would you like for a mate?

A twenty-year-old man may die in a day and a ninety-year-old man may live forever.

3. What height is the man of your dreams?

I'll answer your question with a question: "Why are we measuring mate compatibility based on answers to inherently superficial questions?"

A list of better questions is this:
In your opinion, what was the most important historical event during the 20th century and why?
a. What form of socio-economic organization do you feel is most appropriate for the advancement of technology and science?
b. How does the mass production and sale of animal flesh reflect the culture of the United States?
c. Chiang Kai-scheck or Mao Tse-tung?

She received a reply:

Rachel Synog,

The written part of your profile either requires more practical answers or must be omitted altogether in order for us to process your application. The thirty multiple-choice questions you answered out of the seventy-five should suffice for us to find you a match. Thank you for your interest.

Happy Love,

S.C.M.

But now Rachel met with Horace's ghost.

"Did you know Termer died?"
"Who's Termer?" asked Rachel.
"He's a bloated Babylonian nobleman."

Their ghosts spoke softly in tiny sentences. Each word moved like a delicate breeze that glided through a no B-School summer afternoon. Each was a little hesitant but totally peaceful.

"He is bloated metaphorically?"
"No, literally, like helium lunches."
"People keep dying."
"They will never die."
"We . . . I . . . mean our consciousnesses live on always."
"Our consciousnesses are only a realization of the self at present."
"Our physical structure is not immutable."
"Can that be proven?"
"We are the proof."
"Do these dreary run-down decaying Cleveland buildings have consciousness?"
"You have the answer."
"Consciousness just is. Everything exists, and then when you gain consciousness of it, it exists subjectively."
"Is God the exception?"
"God exists. You are conscious of it. Are you not?"
"I am conscious of the idea of God."
"Are you conscious of the idea of love?"
"Yes, I have felt it."
"You can feel God, too."

The ghosts sorted that kind of stuff out.

Rachel's Dream

The beauty of life is that it is filled with inherent consequences that cripple the spirit of all individuals. It cannot be avoided. We need not seek any revenge anymore. Does she have the kind of brainpower where it is impossible to fit in with a group of standard people? Does she never relate to person X or person C? Does she have that intellectual gift to despise and feel sorry for all? All at once?

* * *

Denny woke up and immediately headed to the door with the energy of a comet. He already had clothes on, some jeans (four straight days), a white tee shirt (three days straight, yellow crust) and a turtleneck from 1990. His hiking boots bled with mountain splinters. He swiftly ran three of his sweaty and greasy fingers through his hair as the only slight act of hygiene he performed on his way out the door.

As he ran up the driveway, his motivation sprayed from his pea-green aura. The sub-conscious of his neighbor down the block could notice it but ignored it to maintain their privacy and apathy. The ground rocked a little and may have crumbled somewhere. Denny was doing something with speed. The prophets who watched could not interpret it. It was an anomaly, unpredictable, and going against the scriptures. How would they explain it to their flock of innocent victims?

He ran, jumped and moved . . . yes, he moved quickly, rapidly, speedily and with haste never previously perceived. His hair flew straight back and hung extended in the air like a dog's tail in a cartoon chase. The wind blew into his shirt and gave it a superhero cape like appearance. He appeared ready to go buy a balloon for Rachel. He moved forward up the driveway motivated. His knees bent, and his legs

106

creaked releasing the rust from so many cobweb afternoons.

Horace had another Pat Beagley dream as the raisin leapt from below the bosom and above the pillars. Roman criminals ran no slower from the den of giant mythical lions with God's hand setting them free.

Denny seemed possessed. He started the car and drove, but as he pulled out, the side of his 1984 Cavalier bumped Termer's Mercedes. The ghost returned with fried chicken spilling from his mouth. He had only been dead for twenty-six hours.

"What happened to my car?" said the ghost of Termer.
"Hi there, Termer! Looks like I hit it accidentally."
"You ain't gonna make it to heaven."
"Why?"
"Because you ruined my car!"

Denny thought to himself, "At least when he was alive, we could distract him with weed and giant portions of greasy unhealthy food. We could avoid him, but now as a ghost, he's impossible to avoid."

Termer's ghost spoke again, "Denny, you don't have a driver's license. You don't have insurance. You don't have a social security number. You don't pay taxes. You indulge in illegal drug use. You want to build a motor that runs on compressed air. You want to build windmills and mine gold and construct enormous domes. You are not fit for this current physical world. Kill yourself like I did! You will never make it to heaven.

Denny's anger forced snots from his nose, and he quickly whirled around and fell unconscious. His collapse brought him ever closer, again, to the small wood worn cracked bleach-stained sediment porch where varieties of frozen meats allowed their scent to float in the smoke of the chipped coral reef-like charcoal pillow. His foot tapped from the far away stereo noise and powerful smoke ventilation. Suddenly, a different sun shone on that "in ground pool escapism mentality." His shirt barely hung onto his skin unbuttoned as he breathed through pores and gills. He ate and swam and smoked marijuana in the sun, but in Virginia, it rained that day, and he never bought the balloon. He wanted so badly to assimilate the memories of his fictitious past life of daydream childhood expectations, but he couldn't.

Sun/Rain/Hot/Cold/Ohio/Virginia

The differences infected his soul like the wormwood cleansing cocktail served at Horace's champagne silver brunch.

The sterno remembrances of flair gun, truck stop, break job agony permeated his muscles. His alcoholic father (Mr. Wister) wore Vietnam War ears coupled with the calculated -meter-four chord-music bar of early rock, and became estranged in a world of endless cigarettes, plump porno pics, and incessant worry about cleaning the top felt of the unused pool table and ping pong court. The ping pong rackets hung on an old tiled Victorian wall where framed pictures of things like Jesus, Boy Scout awards, Football Players, and Air Force planes displayed an "American Dream Motif," as some suburban home decorators called it.
Denny spoke, "The world is falling apart and so are its desires. I no longer desire anything, not even an argument of libertarian construct, not the participation in the forty-five minute bacon and egg preparation, not even the sacrifice of twelve hours in waking life communicating with fellow human beings. Maybe we cannot define human nature. Maybe all is meaningless, but Rachel, my intentions . . . my

intentions are pure. They are as pure as the Nihilism embedded in your soul."

He could hear the phone ring, so he ran into the house. "Horace! Don't answer it! It's Rachel. I can feel it. I can feel her." He stumbled and tripped and knocked things over. "Whachoo runnin' for?" asked the ghost of Termer. Denny finally answered the phone. He did it. He answered.

"Hello There"
"Denny! It's you! You picked up the phone. I've been waiting for this moment for months. I've been imagining what we'd say."
"I am changed."
"The balloon. Have you thought about it?"
"Yes, I have, but I don't think I can make the twelve hour . . ." Denny paused, "I will be there."

The called dropped. The phone rang. Rachel called back. Denny ignored it and picked up some tools.

* * *

"How do I relive a vibration?" Horace asked Denny.
"Oh, I forgot to tell you. I got a letter from Taze."
"Really? Can you read it?"

It read:

Listen guys, we really have to get moving with our music. I was talking to this woman, Akari, and I wrote her this note:

I really hope you have fun. Your life is so very important and relevant to the rest of us. All the fiction will someday cause you to sigh and think for a moment, but, unfortunately, in that moment when you and your brain are finally together, nothing will happen. You will let the moment pass away and buy a drink, some Chai tea, and say something completely and impossibly uncreative.

What did you think? Is she demoralized? I don't care.
She is dead to me.

Anyway, you guys are wasting away. Do you need me
to help organize your shit? Where is Termer? Some
sort of strange vibration told me that you saw his
ghost and that possibly all you guys are now ghosts. Is
this true? Sorry for so many questions. Can I come up
there and stay with you a bit? I need to go to
California eventually and pick up a new Vox organ.
Will one of you drive with me? We can stop in old El
Paso on the way and buy some food and dust. The
palm trees never stop their sway.

Later,
Taze

P.S.-- I took one of those dating exams.

Denny looked at Horace with eyes that dove into his
soul. Horace looked back surprised. "What is it,
Denny?" Denny's mouth opened. In their minds, they
said together:

I take each minute at a time. I cannot cope with
thinking, planning, and reacting to the wide spectrum
of the illusory top-less-ness of capitalist life. It remains
too fast and dangerous for me. I will not conform, not
sell out, or become one of them. I am me, and I will
continue to sit and stare. I will continue to stand in
one place and allow my eyes to blink ferociously and
passionately. I will place my hand face down on the
table and plant a tree every six months, right after the
passing of *Genesis* locusts and *Revelation* frogs. I will
listen to the heartbeats of every inanimate object that
becomes conscious. Consciousness is becoming.
Becoming is consciousness, and existence continues to
baffle. I will respond to fire drill refinement and shake
my fist to the secret dangers of hypocritical laborious
scientific social interaction. I will not fear the body of

110

a woman who shines her hair with television spectacles and digital hard drives. I will meditate somehow and become enlightened without The Tibetans or The Zen Men or The Dharma Bums. Thin, I will stand like a hurricane survivor in a third world disaster.

They stopped talking for a moment. Every instant proved too much for their nerves, and could Taze represent a surrogate savior as a ransom of Rachel's birthday balloon? It could pop. It could explode like Everglades lonely road jeep tire or lonely road soft-top explosion on Route 95. Sadness wasn't the main issue. Efficiency was. That was their main form of criminal activity. Sitting around, and not getting stuff done, like two bears not eating in the fall.

They spoke again:

I will sit and stare. I will reflect the potential possibility of reflecting on the specific action, which is moving around, typing, eating, cooking, walking, picking things up and, most of all, participating.

Horace felt like he could swallow the clouds.

Denny felt like he could gargle angel blood.

Horace felt like he could put his handprint on a canvas and declare it a disaster.

Denny felt the need to put a dab of makeup (foundation) on a blemish.

Horace decided something.
Denny thought.

Horace elbowed the couch cushion unconsciously once and consciously once.

Denny realized, "Jesus needed to be sacrificed."

111

Horace uncovered a bruise in the coffee table.

Horace muttered, "The television is ringing, and I'm watching the phone. The mirror shows no reflection, and I feel bald. My shoe fits like a mitten. My inside is another's outside."

Denny wondered about all this gibberish. "Horace, what did you read?"
"I keep reading and rereading the ancient scrolls of Horacen. I found them moldy in Taze's decayed Cleveland basement."
"I have another letter from Taze. He sent it three months ago." It reads like a poem:

Hey Horace:

Dissolve again in the century mist of prison hole darkness.
Aged distinctly with triangle dance of stars' vision.
We become the material around us and float heavenly.
Stars reflect from our molded mirrored bodies.
We look with emphasis on pleasures' realm.
Existence now not so dreary under the rain of a Caligulous sky.

Anyway, how is your colon fetish? Have you cleansed it? Does that picture of the inflated organ still get you sweating? I just ate some hot sauce and fruit. I drank the number seven. Actually, we need to write songs about the people from the death row steel plant neighborhood of Croom doom. Is that a plan?
How is Denny? Is it working out the way you imagined? I mean, in your relationship with him. You have to keep up any form of mutual respect you can muster. I know when *I* get there, I will cement it all. We will become an art machine and all the cruel dismal business gold sacrifices of your lives will wilt under the silence of art's music. We will all become. Remember that. I think it was Rachel who spoke

112

about that. By the way, she's obsessing about balloons again. So, if she requests one, get it for her.

Got to go,
Taze

"Horace, tell me about you and Taze. How did it happen?"

"Ahh, it's a long myth to be certain. I mean, he . . . or I should say we . . . we . . . ahh . . . we were raised in The Watchtower. Brothers and Sisters filled the Kingdom Hall. We knew only them on Sunday mornings and on almost every weeknight as we trudged our depressed souls to the bricks, lobby, the large room with no windows, and the literature counter. Taze didn't say much at first as he mostly went to the ladies' room with his mother and would hide out on the toilet. Taze danced distinctly at moments when Nancy played a piano song "From House to House" before they used the cassettes, then the CDs. Ahh . . . the disgust and the misery with the innocence of pure people's sincere love. It wasn't conscious in my mind until . . . I mean the entire period of time was a haze until recently when I realized that things were not normal. Most kids didn't ride in a car every Saturday morning with enormous sixty-year-old Polish women smelt with garlic, to preach to their neighbors. Most kids expected to live past eighteen years old and thought of futures of family glory and neighborhood in-ground pool escapism. Most kids didn't spend Tuesday nights engrossed in discussions about why not to accept blood or why not to join the military."

"That's quite a story, Horace."
"There's more. Maybe I shouldn't tell you."
"Is it about Rachel?"

The two continued this discussion even though an incredible amount of work had to be completed in an incredibly short amount of time.

"I have another letter from Taze. Do I dare read it to you?"
"Read Horace."

Taze's letter:

This letter concerns nothing:

Horace, Denny, I am coming soon. I had a more than fretful experience with the Find-a-Mate people at their headquarters. I rambled in a little drunk and slightly unruly, I admit. But in their letter to me it stated that in order for them to 'attach me to some female entity,' I must first give them a blood and urine sample. Apparently, they want to make sure that I have never experimented with LSD or any "psychedelic drugs." They may even want some of my hair. "What do you mean by 'some female entity?'" I want the human species, nothing else; I won't settle for it. They wrote, "What race do you want?" Naturally, I replied, "Worldly."

I am rambling again, but I still keep picturing the way you two argue about gold and picturesque mountain pleasure hot tubs. I really need to get up there away from this traffic and beach and these palm trees and the showy glitter of BMWs. By the way, I ran into Termer's ghost, actually he visited me and said even in heaven he needs Pravastatin.

Later,

Taze

P.S.- The Precambrian insects are at it again.

Horace started speaking again with vigor and vim. "Denny, you must go to Rachel. She is still in Cleveland. Go to her now, please. The balloon is in the room, and the helium machine is clean. Blow it up now, maybe even with oxygen."

So, Denny got up and ran toward the balloon and then to the door but tripped over the foot of Termer's ghost and hit his head on the corner of the coffee table and fell unconscious.

*   *   *

Horace ignored the slight nutation of Denny's head and hair. He himself dozed off into a time-wasting nap. Their dreams synchronized. They sat in a large field of now extinct plants holding long memorial night parking lot flashlights surrounded by unknown peoples. Lighting the pipe had become an ordeal for Denny even with his Boy Scout background of flint and tree bark rope tying manual of vomit tan weekly uniform. But when it was lit and inhaled, the vibratory discussion began with energy and storm force gusto. They spoke to the spirit of Synog.

He said, "You are two of the most depraved and decrepit searchers I have ever encountered. You do not respect the artistic nature of your souls and instead choose a life patterned in extraneous politics."

Denny listened intently, but Horace grew irritated quickly. "I have so much anxiety and it cannot be solved through art alone."

The spirit of Synog continued, "Give up your habits and tendencies. They are your crutch. They are what hold you back from the grace and elegance you lust. Think of the golden refinement of Rachel. She sits quietly with anarchy manuals in hand, ready to help others and give sound advice for revolution. She is prepared to take her cause to death's dreary window of madness and to escape and never return to the

115

normalcy of engagement patterns. She is your hope. The potential of her death alone should be the motivation you need to move. It shouldn't be a question of whether or not she dies. It should be a question of love. How much love do you have in your soul?"

"My soul is empty."

"I know it is. All forms of love that you have known in your life have been conditional. You have never experienced any unconditional love."

Horace came to a realization, "My parents demanded belief in their religion dooms day prophecy of everlasting second death destruction."

"Horace, your mind is a burial chamber of mythic byproducts confused by technological arrogance and printing press immortality. Overcome this hope and believe in death's altruistic riddles of unconscious bliss. Look for my rainbow."

Horace awoke from his nap and saw Denny still unconscious on the floor. Denny continued with the dream sequence.

Denny shed a tear: "The carpet on chilled basement floor 3am scout bed, speaker surround fortress with mirrored ceiling and pipe close by circled mind of last endeavor for financial security. Stars flew from bong resilience of tiny window screen airflow where the neighbors witnessed neck extension disguised fidget smoke breath and ankle split from wobbly chair's fall, ice pick frozen driveway evenings of post potato pancake dinner where cement cracked from weathered eight-month snow depression in former steel production land."

*   *   *

There was no more fiction left for Denny to reconcile, only the harsh truth that Termer's ghost stopped visiting and that Rachel's birthday was less than 24 hours away. He wondered about the sincerity of her

116

lust for suicide, but that thought passed and, as a new one entered, Horace walked in on his gentle friend thinking.

Horace said, "You're going to get in that mobile transport of yours and make it fly?" He understood the importance of Rachel and her connection to them and their survival. Too many chances to make friends and become part of a unified organization passed. Denny became so focused on minute details that he lost his friends and family. "Rachel waits. She left a message on Termer's voicemail."

It said, "Denny! I saw a glorious rainbow this morning. Wonder awaits. I can't reveal to you what that means to me at this point. Just do your best to get here with the balloon."

Denny looked up at Horace with a slight gaze. He could picture the bright sunshine that followed the blackened rainstorm on the thruway through Cleveland. He could see it as vivid as an LSD flashback. The clouds gave way. The tiny puddles melted salty hail. Magnificent colors, all eight perfectly positioned and aligned, comfortably laid next to each other without swirl or haze. The rainbow, maybe the same one Noah saw.

Denny placed himself back five thousand years to sit with fires that smote advancement in technology. He epiphanized life without his computer and discovered the significance of seeing clouds and sun and rain, but for 30 years never seeing the half-circled symbol of God floating in mid-heaven. He pictured poetry of sages concerning God's communication. He took this seriously, and Horace left the room.

Denny felt increasingly alone in his endeavor. It didn't involve repairs for people. It didn't involve adding figures for college prep classes of ten years earlier. It didn't involve a new compartment for some newly purchased screws. It didn't involve folding empty marijuana baggies into small squares. It involved pure action, something for which he did not know the exact reason. Rachel gave him this assignment as the final vestige of her existential dogma. The last thing she would ever tell somebody to do because we are all "condemned to be free."

All of the flashback dissonance from Horace's raving mind finally made sense next to Rachel's message. He noticed Horace falling again to near sleep, a sleep that, if induced, might last 20 hours. So, Denny screamed at Horace, "I understand the concept of Garlinger. I appreciate the historical conditional friendships you shared in the Kingdom Hall. Wake up my friend. We have a fifteen-hour drive through West Virginia mountaintops and Appalachia poverty. Wake up young soul of deck maintenance and free yourself with the balloon of passion from Rachel! Don't you see, Horace? That the balloon is just a symbol of our freedom."

*   *   *

Denny reached down and picked up Horace and got him dressed. They got in the car immediately after blowing up the balloon. Rachel's birthday, 23 hours away, long drive ahead. Two children of a different sun, not the Aztec one or the Navajo one, but the one of redemption never dreamt of in the youth of Denny's Catholic closed-door confessions or Horace's Jehovah's Witness public reproof. They glided down mountains blasted up in the old mining economy.

Horace entered a trance, and Denny noticed and tried to stop it.

"Horace, you have to focus."

Denny saw some blue lights in the rear view.

"Not the cops!" Denny knew he had no driver license and that the Alberta plates on his old Camero were fake. Did he swerve? Did he speed? Was Horace so much of a distraction that he forgot to use his blinker? Denny pulled over and took out a list of questions to ask all traffic cops when stopped.

"Hi there, officer."

"License and registration." The cop was in no mood for a man with long hair in a car that smelled like weed. He repeated, "License and registration."

"I have to plead the 9th amendment to the constitution that states that I have the right to travel."

The cop looked puzzled and said in a heavy southern accent, "What are you talking about son?"

Denny thought quickly and said, "Well, officer, you see, my friend and I have to deliver this balloon for existential reasons to a woman in Cleveland who asked for it. She will commit suicide if she doesn't receive it."

"What in God's gracious name are you talking about?"

Denny clearly noticed that this West Virginian cop never read Sartre. For a split second he thought of handing him a copy of *Being and Nothingness*, but he thought better, and Horace interrupted by singing an old Kingdom melody:

"Cymbals are crashing, white horses thrashing, this is Jehovah's day, let it be nigh."

Denny realized that there was no way to explain Horace's mental health to the cop, but he tried anyway. "This man is in great danger of a nervous breakdown as we speak. Is there an institution close by?"

"I'll tell you what," said the cop, "there ain't no institution, but there is a county jail not more than a stone's throw away. Now give me your license and registration before I give you a piece of southern justice."

This scared Denny. He had been beaten up once before by a cop, but that was by the Cleveland PD, and he knew where he stood with them. But he didn't know what these southern police officers might do. He was relieved to see a sign in the distance that read West Virginia City, Virginia: 3 miles.

The sky opened like another LSD flashback. A loud voice spoke for all three men to hear. "I am Otis Synog. Release these men from bondage. They must preserve the life of my granddaughter. She plans to take her own life. Not to see God but to prove that life is meaningless.

Denny noticed something change in the cop's appearance. The cop actually started to resemble a polar bear. Denny stepped on the gas when he realized that the cop was nothing more than Termer's ghost.

Denny turned up the volume on the cassette. He preferred analog recordings. He sang along allowing the hills of West Virginia to roll by. Horace continued to desperately sing old Kingdom melodies. In order to disrupt Horace's flow, Denny made him read a letter. It was another letter from Taze.

Yo Yo Hannas:

I am sorry Denny. I am an imposter. I am not a Christ figure. I am not Homer Smith. I am not an artist. I am an imposter and a loser. I am caustic. My poems are fiction. It is only my vocabulary that creates these metaphors, not my soul. They don't come from the depths of my inner being but from the very top of my brain, my fucked up brain. I could say I'm sorry, but that would be truly insincere. I don't care about other people. I am bitter and angry and insecure. I could write words in particular order that illustrate metaphorical wonderment, but why? I could write something like:

Brave blades of grass
Sit oppressed never blessed
As folly stands upon lime
In cement time
And trees that otherwise dance
In wind romance
Dangle dead in
Pollutions bed
in steel soil
from mining
of aluminum foil

I can write that stuff anytime I want. I am crude, and I should have a large rounded belly. I don't know why I don't. I would trade my soulless poetic gifts for one single passionate chance at balloon redemption. Here's another:

Flowered see through stockings
Lay unfurled on morning's pillow
And speak of separation
Of man from inhibition's dawn
Checkered textures fall from ceiling's stare
As eyes blink with guilt affair
Couch spring pounces upward
And resounds with coffee splatter

See how easy it is, Denny? Anyhow, how is the drive to Cleveland? I hear there's a storm a brewin'. Has Horace stopped singing Kingdom melodies yet? Write back.

Taze

p.s.- I am only algae now!

*   *   *

Horace sang, "Cymbals are clashing, whitewater splashing, this is Jehovah's day, let it be nigh!"

The snow started to fall heavy in uneventful Ohio. It was around 2am, and they would arrive in Cleveland at around 7am. "What is this then, Horace?"

Horace sat and couldn't think hard enough to answer. Then suddenly he spoke, "This is the journey to the beginning of the day!"
"You sound optimistic?"
"No, just the opposite. All great deeds occur at night when ugliness is hidden in darkness behind clouds and dim moonlight."

NEXT:

Rachel couldn't sleep. Detached from family, she didn't know how to prepare for her birthday. She had renounced the close-knit nuclear family institution long ago preaching a belief in the Iroquois confederacy longhouse family arrangement. Her mother dead. Diane, Otis, all of them dead. Cikota's butler entered the room and asked her a question, "Are you ready for your birthday?" Rachel did not answer. She looked into the cloudy rust belt sky. She understood that Cleveland died years ago, just another refugee from the factory generation.

A light snow started and began to cover everything in what she recalled as "white death." a famous Cleveland blizzard expression.
"Otis, Otis, Otis . . .daylight decides visions divine."

She felt unable to keep her promise to her grandmother, despite the godly poetry. Denny had to arrive with the balloon on time, in the right place, on the right day, in the correct context, with the right breath, with the soft kiss, with the sun, not snow, with Synog's rainbow.

*   *   *

Horace as a passenger proved useless, no navigation skills, usually sleeping, and this time his hummus recipe eeeeked into the conversation. "Just add olive oil, lime, garbanzo beans, and paprika and blend." The only problem is that he blended too much and destroyed the blender's motor. The noise of it, the second before it blew, that's the noise he heard from Denny's Camero engine. A hiss from the snake with a chortle from the Egyptian Mau, he perceived just under the layers of wind, music, vent and wiper blades, and Horace recognized it because it grew necessary for survival. He could envision it dead in an Ohio back town. As hard as he tried to muster a picture in his mind of a suburban neighborhood without snow and with basketball nets swaying, he just couldn't. He saw rotted manufacturing and sewers upside down. His mind generated sludge attached to battery caps and salt pellets stitched to exhaust pipes. He imagined dark black tornado smoke. He saw bathrooms without a fan or towel and only a thin toothpick like a sliver of light-green dried soap.

He dreamt of gas station coffee where viruses clung to mixing sticks and sugar particles and where seats showed more cushion than pleather, and the pleather was a red invented and discontinued in the year 1975 (Henry Ford Red).

Denny took the curve of the hill at 80 mph and the car started to spin. It swirled and, from the sky above, planes or anything looking down could probably see a t-top descending, not over the side of the cliff, but into a hole in the road. Pure white snow flickered from the tires in every direction. It pinwheeled. The dizziness set in as both men fell unconscious and a strong sound of the sitar started transcending, emanating through the hill up through the bottom of Denny's car. The

123

electricity of the sound penetrated their skin and flesh and entered their bones into the marrow and further into the cells. It explored their brains and although their skulls were completely still, their brain stems vibrated sending messages to the front of the skull.

A poem exited Denny's mouth:

The calendar sky
The moon cannot lie
The sun will decide
This fateful drive

This canyon below
This siphon of snow

A poem exited Horace's mouth:

Tablets for Holy Zion are filled
By seers of hillside plunge
Inscribed not written
Inerasable
Divine finger chalk
The final plague
Is written
In apathy and
Is apathy

Lines kept flowing in and out and in and out again as the car flew through underground tunnels.

Magicians rumble rabbit's tail
Cone hats with crescent moons
Wands of belindas
Stars on corner pillows
Cats in tunnels
brave pillars of Samson
Book
Sand

Gaping
Knelt
Spray.
Hu
Jah
Opp
Shh
K

"Rachel is already dead," Denny exclaimed as both men noticed that the car stopped its spin. The car faced north, and they continued to travel to Cleveland, balloon intact.

*   *   *

Rachel paced in her room like in some high school production of a soliloquy. "The baker shall be hung from a tree. The birds shall eat the flesh of the baker. Just three generations ago we celebrated the special days of Job's children. But grandma and mom forbade this activity . . . this birthday activity. And now her dreams tell her that some shall die. Some shall be eaten by birds and digested in stomach acids.

Frigid air as darkness dims
As daylight decides visions divine
As hollowed trees scream
And the baker will die and be murdered in cold blood
as cold blood slides through ice and mud

She said all of this to God and read her *My Book Bible Stories.*

She said to herself, "Of course, I'm mad! Do you understand the confusion of my childhood as an intellectual with the prospects of world's end on any random day? Of course, I'm mad. All of the elements of theocracy are oppressive." Rachel entered a deep mind jungle with mosquitoes and tiny poison frogs. Her birthday elegance contradicted a lost belief system . . . lost in grandmother's death. "Is death the end of consciousness? Perhaps I should experiment. Perhaps I should manifest some sort of King Herod romanticism? Is John the baptizer approaching?"

Rachel walked slowly outside into the cold spinal tingle of the winter morning and thought about the drive to her own birthday party. People she barely knew organized this event in her honor. They figured it might cheer her up considering the recent death of her grandmother.

But Rachel wasn't anywhere near ready for the embraces of strangers, even if they approached her with unconditional agape love. She only wanted to attend the party to see Denny. She missed him and, somewhere in her soul, she may have even loved him. She may have loved his complete lack of reliability and punctuality. She may have loved his obsessive-compulsive behavior. She may have even loved his giraffe like posture. She certainly admired his lack of a cell phone, his organic garden, his incessant pot smoking, his expertise of computers, car engines, guitars and keyboards, juice machines, and law. There were so many reasons to love him or to at least forgive him.

* * *

"SURPRISE!!!" The entire assembled group screamed together. Rachel looked around the room, one by one examining the people.

1. Garlinger- 87-year-old man who embraced Russlite philio-religion in 1931.
2. Reese- Use of jerry curl predated Randall Cunningham.
3. Pat Beagley- Dead
4. Gary Grandin- Brown shoes pointed at the end, leisure suit, and auto mechanic mustache with mustard stain in the center.

Rachel's head continued in a slow circular motion.

5. Richard- Favored the Terry Bradshaw look in men's hair.
6. Suthowski- Drunk with giant red nose, Cornell graduate in history, emphasized the importance of water.
7. Sikota- Drew lines across the top of her eyes as artificial brows, smelled like freshly juiced garlic.
8. Donna Panzerelle- tall, thin, and beautiful. Horace's first crush, ten years his elder.

Rachel stood confused because she knew that all of these people never celebrated birthdays. They all belong to The Watchtower. She thought that maybe a wish fulfillment dream manifested before her eyes. Then she quickly thought of the Pharaoh's baker and John the Baptizer's head. "I need to get out of here." When she did not see Denny in the small dingy perogy ladened room, she looked down at the worn plaid carpet.

She looked up and spoke, "Who are you people? I don't know you. I realize that your love is real, but maybe that sort of love is, after all, fiction." She looked over and saw several gifts stacked up to the low discolored popcorn ceiling. "At least open your gifts," said Sikota. The gifts:

1. Pinstriped wrapping paper- markers, colored pencils and stencils in a box that said, "Be an artist, draw your own shapes."
2. Poster with an aerial view of Cleveland. Plain black.
3. A globe that still had the U.S.S.R.

Other gifts weren't as significant as those. Finally, at the bottom of the pile sat an envelope. When she opened it, the people seemed to close in on her like in a kindergarten reading circle. Inside the envelope was yellow crusty paper.

She read:

Death's agony
brilliance in death
I, too, believe in Him
The one sent forth
To profess
eye in your name
To commit miracles
Oh, death doesn't end anything
God will meet you
Bestow luxury ambiguously
Upon you
Perhaps an unfortunate
continuance of spirit
For souls discontent
Perhaps rambling
Discordance of beliefs structures
Don't worry Rachel, it will end soon
Suicide I committed off the bridge

Rachel slumped. "So, who redeems suicide? Life and death is pure meaning. Both are meaning. No balloon. Maybe, I will die today. Mercy be shown. Forgive me, Jehovah."

*   *   *

Denny dropped off Horace at the sign that called Cleveland, an "All-America City." The winds and snow continued to pile up as the sun started its ascent over the horizon. He pictured the tear that would cautiously creep down from Rachel's eye over her tender cheekbone to smear her make up and to eventually land in a cavern of dimples. His slide off the road would be similar, a careful and petrified leap for grace.

From a distance, Horace could see the Camaro hanging in the air and a fragile being sitting inside with the face of a monument and with the strong obvious features of a giant statue carved for ancient worship, with the complacency and contentment of Rama.

The auto fell like a parachute through skyway bridge guardrail. The guardrail, an entrance to infinity, and through the ice, the car sank.

*   *   *

Rachel walked deliberately to the center of the ice-covered Lake Erie alone. The entire city was shut down and devoid of any activity at all. Roads had no cars and light signals were black. Ships at the port appeared as breakable as glass, and the naked trees did not move and sat as still as old Pompeii vessels. There was no wind, and with each breath, an invisible shivering stillness stood.

A polar bear appeared and said, "This is for you. It's from Denny."

Rachel took the small note. It read:

DAYLIGHT DECIDES VISIONS DIVINE!

Part 4- "I drink alone." (Early 2007)

They sat in the diner or actually a chic sort of modern coffee café and talked. He just returned from a trip to Los Angeles, and now on the East side of Richmond, they talked. Both were smart, tall, and nervous. They chatted. She had some optimism about the future. He had a death complex.

"You see Akari, I see no reason to continue."
"But what about love? Can't you . . .?"
"I don't trust people. People are organic matter who inconsequentially float from meaningless situation to meaningless situation."
"I understand Taze." She didn't flinch at Taze's dim pessimism. She never showed a sign or a trifle concern at his suicidal plans and thoughts. Taze passed it off as an underlying apathy. He met enough people that seemed to care for a minute but didn't the next."
"You see, Akari, it's just that I think the idea of the family in modern America or, modern anywhere for that matter, is completely artificial. Completely unnecessary, and I think that evolution will lead us to a family structure where we no longer are connected emotionally with the woman who just happened to give birth to us or a man that planted a seed."
"Okay, I see," said Akari. She went with the flow of his treatises unmoved and accepted of everything. She didn't shrink back or excitedly participate. She just kept smiling.
"Don't you think you might be able to ever trust somebody?" asked Akari.
"No, probably not."
"Okay, well. How was Los Angeles?"
"It started off really fun, but you know how things are. By the end of the trip, I was miserable. I just don't think I can enjoy anything anymore."

131

"Nothing?"

"Well, ahhh . . . maybe temporarily."

"Everything is temporary."

Taze smiled back and let down his guard as a waiter brought two more glasses of cabernet.

Taze looked forward to his alienated midnight. Every night for the past six weeks, he thought of the dizzying kiss she'd given him. He'd think of her daring approach where her scent floated like honeyed clouds toward him. He noticed that her feet never left the ground, but instead, they seemed to ride on a mysterious invisible conveyor belt, and gradually with tempting certainty, her lips touched his.

*   *   *

He made his plans almost four years earlier as he rotted in the cantina border city of El Paso, Texas when he began to wake up from the sleep perpetrated by the Watchtower Corporation. He reflected on his life growing up as a Jehovah's Witness.

"I was wondering if I could go to the ice rink."

"Sure, we'll all go. The whole family . . . after our bible study. Did you finish studying your Watchtower for the meeting on Sunday?

"Ahhh . . . actually, I wanted to go to the rink with some friends."

"Are they worldly friends? You know what the bible says about worldly friends, don't you? It says they spoil useful habits."

"But I really want to go with my friends from school."

"Taze, you shouldn't have any worldly friends at school. They are only acquaintances. Get your copy of the Watchtower and read it."

Taze married an often-depressed Jehovah's Witness. She had been a victim of child sex abuse in her Watchtower congregation, but her elders didn't tell the local police and covered up the entire thing at the

132

direction of the leadership of The Watchtower corporation.

Taze was only twenty-three, and she just turned twenty-one when they married. Common ages to be married in The Watchtower.

Taze sat by his bed thinking of memories inspired by his conversation with Akari.

"You could save me, Akari."
"That role is not reserved for me. You can only save yourself."

Akari drank almost every night and sometimes called Taze for drunk late-night conversation.

"You could save me."
"I can't save you. Only you can save yourself. Everybody is alone. Everybody has to live with their emotional demons. Choose to be happy. Don't choose misery. It just seems like you've chosen misery over happiness."
"Akari, I think one person can save another."
"I know, but why do you need to be saved?"

At this point in the conversation, he thought of the plan he conceived in El Paso after he split from his Jehovah's Witness wife and mentally left The Watchtower. He planned to take his own life.

*　　　*　　　*

Akari called one night.

"Hey Taze! It's me, your savior! It's Christ, and I'll baptize you tonight. You're not the only one who needs saving. One time I took five Xanax and snorted five lines of coke hoping I wouldn't wake up."

The next day he met Akari. She approached him wearing very high black heels and slacks with pinstripes. For Taze this moment represented the first fingernail size hope he saw in many years.

"Hi," she said with a smirking smile.
"Hi, um . . . hi. So, where are we going? Did you plan anything?"
"Well, since I know the area well, I did. We're going to an Indian restaurant for Indian food. You do like Indian food, don't you?"
"Ahhh . . . yes. I haven't had it in a while."
"You'll like it. I know you will. One time, about three years ago, I drank bottle of wine at this restaurant, and I spilled some yellow curry all over this guy. I think his name was Amin or something like that. I couldn't go back for a few months."

Taze laughed.

"Yeah, I break and spill things a lot," she said.
"That's pretty funny."

The waiter brought out several bottles of beer for Akari. She drank down all of them. Akari paid.

"I'll pay the bill." She said and her jaw seemed to be collapsing as she spoke. She recognized that Taze noticed and mentioned, "When I was about fourteen, I had a really bad skiing accident. I had some major dental work and some surgery on my mouth. I had to teach myself to speak again correctly, and when I drink, sometimes I speak out of only one side of my mouth. It's sort of embarrassing."
"No, I didn't notice a thing."

They walked together down the streets of Richmond. Neither person touched. Taze too nervous, and Akari too wobbly from beer.

A couple days later they met again.

"Let me see if I can explain this correctly," Taze said, "It's not that I want to die, it's just that I feel life is not worth living. Every good pleasure is transient and is fleeting. That's why I keep myself blank. Fear of emotions."

"Taze, you can choose to be happy. It seems like you want to be miserable, and if that's how you want to be, you're more than welcome to be miserable. More than welcome."

"Akari, I can't just become happy. I'm full of desperate longings and fears. This whole world is new to me. I was a Jehovah's Witness for so long. It's all I really know."

"Sometimes I think . . ."

"Listen Akari, I have this plan, but before I tell you about it, let me explain two things to you. Okay, Akari, listen, I ahhh . . . you see misery fuels my artwork, my writing, and, also, I have a very deep philosophical knowledge of misery and what lies at the soul of man."

"Philosophy is all bull shit. I read Wordsworth's *Preface*. All you have to do is just decide to be happy."

*   *   *

Taze sat alone crushed with negative feelings. His memory brought him to his childhood dinner table where Taze thought, "Please don't ring, please don't ring, please don't ring."

Earlier that day in school, he gave a girl his phone number. "Please don't ring, please don't ring." His aunt sat right next to the phone during dinner. Taze figured he could get the phone if it wasn't during dinner and somehow sneak a five-minute conversation with the worldly girl.

"Please don't ring, please don't ring, please don't ring."

His aunt asked, "So Taze, how was school?"

"Fine." Taze was an exceptional student, very high grades, advanced curriculum.

"You're such a great student. Think about how you can use that intelligence for Jehovah. You can pioneer. Go to ministerial training school. Bethel. You can be a missionary."

The phone rang, and before Taze could move a millimeter, his aunt held the phone in her.

"Hello."

"Is Taze there?" The poor girl meekly asked.

"Taze?"

Taze thought to himself, "Oh damn. Please don't."

"He's in the middle of supper. And may I ask who's calling?"

"My name is Jessica. I'm a friend of his from school."

"Hi Jessica, I'm Taze's aunt. What sort of relationship do you and Taze have?"

Taze thought, "Oh no! Here is comes."

"What sort of relationship do you have with Taze?"

"Ahhh . . . we're good . . ."

Taze thought, "Please don't say were good friends."

"We're good friends."

"Oh really."

"Yes. We talk every day. Taze is really a great guy."

Taze looked down at his untouched food and somehow it shrunk on the plate before his eyes.

His aunt got off the phone and started on Taze, "What was that all about? A worldly girl calling here. Having a girl call here to talk. Is she your girlfriend? Don't even think about living a double life. Jehovah knows. He reads hearts."

*   *   *

Akari approached.

"Hi Akari. How are you?"

"I don't feel so great, I slept really late because I drank two bottles of this Spanish wine. I like it soooo much."

"Well, you could have called to cancel. I mean, I hate to make you stay out when you're not feeling well."

They entered a small Italian restaurant, and she asked for a booth in the back of the restaurant.

"I don't like olives, peppers, hot pepper, jalapenos, mushrooms, sausage, pepperoni, onions, ham, pineapple or sausage on my pizza," said Akari.

"Okay. Let's just get cheese."

Akari drank two quick glasses of wine and elbowed a piece of pizza to the floor. Her elbow print was engraved into the cheese and a circular stain of grease remained on the floor.

"I always do stuff like that. I spill things and break things a lot."

"That's alright. It was funny."

"I have to finally be honest with you Taze. My father demands a lot of me. My mother goes along. They're actually disappointed with me because I studied poetry in college. Does that make any sense? They're disappointed because I am a college professor. Does that make any sense?"

"No. I don't think so."

"It doesn't. Believe me. They wanted me to be a doctor."

"My aunt wanted me to be a circuit overseer."

Then she held up her glass of wine and moved it toward her mouth and, with a slightly angry look in her eye, said, "Don't judge me. I drink to escape."

Taze didn't respond at all. He just looked at the pizza. Akari seemed to instantly snap out of her sudden anger.

"So, are you excited about Los Angeles?"
"Well, yeah, a little. I mean I think it will start off really fun but then, like everything else, it will sort of dissolve into some kind of depression."
"Why do you set yourself up for failure?"

Taze thought about his plan that he created in El Paso.

Akari repeated, "Why do you set yourself up for failure?"

This question brought Taze back to a memory of his wife.

"Taze, you have to answer at the book study. It just looks bad when you don't answer. You just sit there in a daze. What's wrong with you?"

"Hello, Taze, I am asking why do you set yourself up for failure."
"Oh, I don't know. I just haven't had much success in a lot of ways."

Neither of them ate any of the cheese pizza.

They went to a Mexican restaurant, and Akari ordered a bottle of beer with lime, and, when inserting the lime, she spilled one fourth of the beer on the table and a little in her lap. Taze laughed.

"I spill stuff and knock stuff over sometimes."
"That's cool. I like it."

She ordered a burrito and cheese enchilada, and he didn't feel like eating at all. The nauseating depression was a little too strong that day, and he just couldn't bring himself to eat or to talk much.
"I'm really sorry I'm not talking much."

"You're fine, Taze. I mean what do you want to do, keep talking and talking and talking like some motor mouth."

Taze loved to hear her talk and just sat back and listened to her stories. He found them both interesting and almost unbelievable, but he trusted she was telling the truth.

"I fell asleep a lot during class when I was in college, but that's the only time I can just fall asleep, otherwise, I just stayed awake. I never get hangovers. You really must visit Japan. I want to take you there. I was meant to meet you. I feel it was destiny. You really need to stop driving yourself crazy. I remember one time I ate so many schrooms at this concert that I thought I wasn't going to come back to sanity. I thought I'd have to explain to my father that I lost my mind. There are so many things from my past that I could never tell anybody . . . accept maybe you."

Akari kept talking and drinking, and Taze started to think to himself "If this is my savior, I am destined to kill myself." Some very small doubts crept in slowly. But just then Akari stood up and sat down on the other side of the booth, right next to Taze, and gave him a tender kiss on the cheek.

"We were meant to meet each other."
"Are you going to save me?"
"I already answered that question. I cannot save anybody. If you want to kill yourself, then go ahead."
"It's just that I have this plan. This insane plan of dropping out of society and my life and then killing myself."
"I'm drunk," Akari said proudly and went into a sprawling oration and discourse on the beauty of drunkenness. "I drink every night. I drink two entire bottles of wine some nights plus a couple of beers." She smiled, "I was so wasted yesterday that I think I

139

blacked out at some point because when I woke up my arm was still asleep and behind my neck. I had to use my other arm to pick it up and place it on my stomach. One of my toes was a little red and swollen, so I guess I must have stubbed it, but I don't fucking remember."

She continued, "My roommate was doing some early morning cleaning and blamed me for vomiting, but I think she was full of shit. There was also this small bruise on my arm," she pointed to it. "That's attractive, isn't it? I remember once a couple years ago how I ate some LSD and drank a fifth of vodka before 9am, and then I went to a local gas station, and the guy behind the counter made some sort of moral decision not to sell me a case of beer that I desperately needed. He stared at my ID and asked me for my address, which I messed up on, and gave me a short lecture on how drinking is dangerous for the liver. Did you know I have terrible kidneys. My doctor said I have the kidneys of a sick sixty-year-old woman." She took another drink. "Do you like Portuguese wine? I love Spanish wine. In fact, well, here, this is for you." Taze saw a bottle a Portuguese wine on the table. "I want you to drink the entire bottle on . . . I mean in one night while you're in California. I wanted to give you something that means a lot to me. That's sort of part of me."

Taze loved the gift.

"And here, this is my favorite lip balm, I'm addicted to it."

Under the table her leg rubbed against his, and her eyes squinted under the lenses of her glasses. Her lips seemed to purse, and her voice lowered to a more seductive tone. Taze wanted to kiss her. He didn't care about her drinking.

Just then Akari's phone rang. She ignored it. It rang three more times. She finally answered, and it was her mother. It was an emergency. She had to leave.

Taze left Los Angeles the next day.

Los Angeles, California

He sat on the beach with beer. He rubbed his hand deep into the sand for seashells and other remnants of Japan that may have crossed the ocean.

An old ex-JW friend of his picked him up earlier.

"Dude, you made it! You want to smoke?"
"Ahhh . . . no, I don't think so, sometimes it makes me think too much and then I end up in a stupor."
"Okay, I get it, grab a beer then, it's in that cooler."
They went straight to Venice Beach.
"What are we doing?"
"I don't know what you're doing, but I'm surfing."

So, Taze sat on the beach. He thought of Akari, but quickly brushed the thought out of his mind. Her abuse of alcohol bothered him greatly, and he didn't want to end up sitting in a corner or under a pier wishing for death because of his inherent inability to cope. Taze sat motionless.

His ex-JW friend interrupted, "Dude, we're gonna get some fish tacos?"

Taze wrote a poem in his head:

Arteries of distant rivers flow with wooden rafts floating one inch above water, and in that space

141

between the raft and the water, sits a consciousness holding up and supporting, begrudgingly, the rafts path downstream wishing it would be crushed by rain water, rise of river or wooden plummet, but there it lies without a legitimate hope because without it, the raft and river would not exist and only the sun opens up his consciousness through its evaporating powers as waters and memories change molecularly and transform to images of mountain tops and walks up pathways that are beams of light and helplessness goes the way of water vapor and wood rots and decays freeing the soul of his consciousness and the only ascension he'd ever dream of could possibly be a reality, but she must be by his side, hand in hand, riding the beam to sunlight breaking the clouds that become purple unable to separate hands touch.

Slight sprinkle of ocean mist dabs Taze's toes with childish innocence and asks for some slight recognition as if saying, "look down into the infinite and blue beauty of the ocean, stop gazing bravely into the sun, its burn may be soothed by ocean waters. Its brightness may be dimmed by waves of bubbly floating sands and only at the horizon, at dusk, may we meet to fulfill hope. Only at that point when beauty meets nightly beauty can your eyes focus and understand that everything is around you, and it is she who meets the sun and ocean at dusk."

Taze wanted so badly to see dusks clarity provided from heavens brilliance and only he knew at that moment on that sand, that it Akari who is heaven, and it is Akari the provider hope.

He walked away from the beach and sat on a stool in bar where his ex-JW friend ate fish tacos with thick chunky salsa on a waxy surfboard table. "Taze, what's up? Man, you're zonin' out today. What's on your mind?"

142

"Not sure if I could explain it concisely. I get into these moods. You seem happy. How do you do it?"

"My dad wasn't a J-dub. I got to make my own choices. Came out west and try to just chill most of the time."

"Yeah. I know. Makes sense. I remember how you had choices, and how your mom was a really laid-back witness."

"It makes a difference bro."

"Well, you see, I met this woman."

"What's she like? Worldly right?"

"Yes, worldly. She's hard to explain."

"Is she hot?"

"Well, yes. But you know, like, that's not the thing. She's really smart. She's a professor. People love her."

"Well people love you, too. I love you buddy!"

Richmond, Virginia

They sat in the diner or actually a chic sort of modern coffee café and talked. He just returned from a long trip to Los Angeles, and now on the East side of Richmond, they talked. She was quite a bit more optimistic than he.

"You see Akari, I see no reason to continue."

"But what about love? Can't you . . .?"

"I don't trust people. People are organic matter who inconsequentially float from meaningless situation to meaningless situation."

"I understand Taze."

She went with the flow of his treatises unmoved and accepted everything. She didn't shrink back or excitedly participate. She just kept smiling.

"Don't you think you might be able to trust somebody ever?" Akari asked.

"No, probably not."

"How was Los Angeles?"

"Okay, it started off really fun, but you know how things are. By the end of the trip, I was miserable. I just don't think I can enjoy anything anymore."

"Nothing?"

"Well, ahhh . . . maybe temporarily."

"Everything is temporary."

Akari's phone rang, and she said she had to leave.

Taze couldn't let her walk away so easily. So, he followed her.

He looked into a bar, and she ordered a drink. Her legs hung like ropes ready for someone to climb. Her smile killed the dim lighting and jazz groove of the smooth sensation sax and tiny snare pops. Her heels like ladders to a fiery sky rise condo, and Taze sad and desperate. She slid off her bar stool with martini glass in hand, and it crashed, causing it to break, cutting her fingers. Blood dripped and then flowed. Taze ran into the bar and lifted her head off the ground.

"I spill things and break things a lot."

The blood from her hand matched the red of her dress, and as Taze held Akari's head in his hands, he whispered in her ear, "Akari. Akari. Akari." She looked up and stared into his eyes and muttered almost incoherently, "You saved me Taze. You saved me."

"But your hand, Akari, it's bleeding."

"Oh Taze . . . it's just a splinter."

Part 5- "I'm a spy in the house of love." (Mid-2007)

The man looked like Santa Claus without the beard and hat. His hand shook with uninsured nervousness as he handed Taze five hundred dollars in cash. Five clean new bills. Taze had an alcohol buzz from the energy malt liquor he discovered a week earlier. Actually, Akari introduced him to it. They left Richmond in a rush and began to travel together with unsecured, unearned funds, driving reckless on unplanned roads, and drinking heavily as they embraced the excitement of their future.

The Grand Canyon lay in the distance, a vast contrast to the shaky plump hand that waved cash in front of Taze. Akari barely contained her laughter. She knew Taze most likely caused the slight fender bender. They collected the money and jumped in and sped off in Akari's father's BMW. She took it without telling him. She just left a note.

The cd player blared The Brian Jonestown Massacre. Her legs hung halfway out the window as they flew past tourists singing along and waking up nocturnal wildlife. She sang out of tune, and he sang with a deep purposeful tone.

When they arrived at the canyon, Akari became obsessed with a lonely yellow fire hydrant which seemed out of place. She took fourteen pictures of it from different angles.

"Let's get a drink. This canyon must have a bar somewhere."

Later Akari thought of the conversation at the gay bed and breakfast, Star Bright Pines, from earlier that day. Pete and Peter were from West Hollywood. Pete, a carefree accountant, bragged about working four hours a week and walking their two shiatsus. Peter wrote and published educational manuals on how to teach non-English speakers the English language. Pete dove into the egg block for breakfast but could not get the bacon due to Peter's implication that Pete had gained too much weight. Peter's ponytail hung like a perfect curl, long and flowing like the Colorado River. Pete mentioned hiking down into the canyon "if there was a tiki bar at the bottom." Everybody laughed heartily.

Taze and Akari sat at the table. They carried on with a casual fun-loving conversation while they held each other as they ate the egg brick, passing on the bacon because Akari didn't eat meat. They wore matching yellow shirts, her shirt a v-neck low cut tee, his a button-down cotton style, both wore large dark brown sunglasses that comfortably masqueraded their very little sleep and constant alcohol consumption eyes.

The canyon bartender, Jack, spoke in a squeaky Midwest accent. His hair dangled to the sides and hung as straight as uncooked Thai noodles. He wasted glassfuls of beer with every draught pour. "Whatta have?" he asked. The two travelers just laughed. They a shared kiss after kiss, and the bartender asked, "Honeymooners?" They looked at each other and laughed again. "Two screwdrivers, Kettle One vodka." Two more drinks. Bartender spoke, "Whereyya from?" They laughed again but answered this time.

Akari spoke up, "We're from Hollywood."
"Hollywood? Whattya do?"
"We're writers." She tipped down her sunglasses, "I write poetry. He writes novels."
"Poetry? What kind? What's it about?"

Akari looked for a second with her hand on her chin and thought. Most of the time her answers to questions came natural and quick, her wit and intelligence obvious and easy.

The last time she answered the poetry question was in Venice Beach at a small hollowed out bar where they sat near the back on a sofa that needed reupholstering.

"So, what is your poetry about?"
"It's about escaping depression, becoming whole, becoming . . . becoming a real person . . . ascending to artistic glory. Picture it as Anais Nin meets Henry Miller."

They raced from a small organic restaurant in Richmond, Virginia to the large bookstore running into the line and getting the books. They ordered the same book with the letters between Miller and Nin. They ran out into the street, pretty much drunk. Then, they sat at an outdoor bar wearing large white sunglasses drinking screwdrivers and Jack shots, and the man next to them asked, "What's your story?"

"We're writers" she said. She wore a long orange and yellow checkered dress. She stood high above the bar stool.
"Writers . . . you look like Hollywood."

They laughed and followed the man into an empty parking lot. Taze rolled a Bugler joint and attempted to steal some pot from the man. The man saw and said, "You're passin' that the wrong way, my friend."

They walked home but made a stumbling stop into an organic co-op to buy Orange Juice.

"Drinking this? It's like injecting Vitamin C directly into your veins."

Akari loved that juice. They stumbled home, collapsed on the bed, and blacked out.

The next time she wore that dress was in Agua Prieta, Mexico.

Roving Mariachis performed at their table.

The multicolored accordion of one of the musicians seemed only to eeeck out a slight sound when pumped. Another musician wore average street clothes in contrast to the traditional costumes the others wore.

Back to Star Bright Pines in the mountains of northern Arizona, Taze made last minute reservations at an internet café in downtown drugged out Fremont Street Vegas coffee shop. The gamblers and beggars saw his enthusiasm, and he provided some safe change for their half-gloved hands. She stood behind him.

"Wow, this looks quaint and cozy. Doesn't it Akari?"
"Oooo, cozy, look at the fireplace, seems Victorian, I mean Romantic to me. Oh. Oh . . . Let's read some Wordsworth tonight."

They sometimes spoke to each other in sprinter phrases, quick and direct.

"Where's my phone?" Akari lost it and became peaceful and relieved, "Great! No calls from Korthoff, Parks, or Grillo."
"Ahh, *Friends*, Beach Boys, I love that."

Then Big Sur to see Country Joe McDonald play one of his six shows of the year. Atop mountain winery, she wore a glamorous dress with tall heals and slowly walked down plank board stairs holding two bottles of wine in plastic to go seven eleven style cups. They danced, and he dipped her.

"That dress looks like the *Wild Honey* album cover" said to the older librarian couple.

Akari spoke, "We're writers, and you should look up our books. Mine is called *Severed Thighs*."

"Oh yes, I heard of that, it's famous."

A tattooed clad man who sat drunk outside a Hollywood Beach, Florida bar also heard of the actually unpublished *Severed Thighs* poetry book. He talked about Akari's book, and Akari smiled and shook her head up and down. "Yes, it has sold many copies, many many copies," she said confidently.

He replied, "I read *Severed Thighs*. Reminded me of Rimbaud."

They took a picture atop Country Joe mountain, and Taze drove, swirling down cliffs, overlooking the great lighted valley. So, this is where they grow all those grapes and make massive quantities of all that wine that we drink almost every night. They discovered the Bandito Brand Wine. Sold in small boxes, full flavored Cab or Merlot for only $8.99.

Akari spoke to Don, the owner of small establishment in Big Sur while Taze spoke to Don's photographer friend. Taze then sat with Don's web designer. They looked at his web page.

A dreamy sunny surf song loop played and played over and over. Don said to Akari, "I make all the food here, designed the menu, the bar, the barbeque, the patio, everything. Would you like to go to a party tonight?"

"Sure, let me ask my boyfriend."

"Taze, would you like to go to a party tonight?"

"I was just invited to the same one. I hear they're recording a band there."

"Sunshine and the Adventure Collection of Pop."

The point of the pine tree meant so much more to Akari with the light of several specific stars shining on it beyond a small nervous crying session. She held Taze tight by the hand.

Back in the car with strange rocks to the sides through Texas Canyon and Continental Divide on the way to El Paso from Sedona. Lounge pizza and vodka recommended by Pete at egg brick breakfast. He had to whisper the recommendation because Peter sat in ear's range. "He wouldn't let me have it but try the pizza. It looked delicious."

Akari had a breakdown and couldn't drive. Caffeine malt liquor heartbeat mixed with adrenochrome, stirred, swallowed, driven through the veins to the heart. Brain power tics, arugula sandwich. "Why don't you eat that?" It sat sweating in the back seat for eight hours, portabella shrinking, bread digested. It had almost become an organism, but Taze encouraged her to eat. He didn't know why, maybe because he didn't want it to go to waste. She listened.

They stopped at rest stops frequently to take bathroom breaks because of the amount of alcohol they consumed on the road. The darkness above yielded a gigantic harvest moon mixed with static lightening flowing through the clouds like brain nerve cells that connected to the desert breeze. They held hands and stared up for a moment. He turned to her, "This is why we are alive, to live these seconds. El Paso will be the same place tomorrow, but we . . . we are here. This shouldn't have happened, me and you, yet it *is*. It exists, we can touch right now and remember it later." He looked into her eyes.

"Tomorrow?"

Akari almost slid across the sandy concrete walkway, that noise, the only one for miles. Taze walked ahead, and she yelled lightly, "You know, we're the only ones out here. We're the only people that exist. El Paso may have sunk. Las Cruces may have burned down. Maybe all the people fled to Juarez or maybe that place is dead too."

Taze stopped his walk, "The world is dead. We are the only thing that is alive."

They felt alone again on this trip atop a roof at a before party for the Persian film festival. One skill Taze held was the ability to look many different ethnicities. His dark curly hair and olive skin made him Middle Eastern, Latin, and Mediterranean.

"So, where are you from?"
Taze didn't know how to answer, "Umm . . ."
"What country are you from?"
"Uhh . . . the United Arab Emirates." Taze mispronounced the country's name badly.
"Well, at least you're from a rich country. And your girlfriend?"
"She's Japanese."
"Oh."

They each bought a jack neat and stood in the chilly air absorbing the lights of downtown San Francisco.

"How did you find out about this event?" Akari asked.
"I overheard some people and now we're here on this roof, looking at Golden Gate in the Tenderloin after Indian kabob cuisine, Moroccan wine bottle, belly dancer, and strange small multicolored vested waiter."

Akari wore a mink collared coat, red cashmere, and walked along late Haight evening, near jazz club, drank sangria laced orange.

They shot from Surprise, AZ to Las Vegas after being asked to leave the house of an old JW friend of Taze. His friend's wife felt a little nervous seeing Akari drink a beer at eleven am. The worldly vibe disturbed the submissive wife.

They sat at a tiny run-down restaurant near Wickenberg.
"So where do we go now? What do we do now? Do we stay in Phoenix?"
"What's there to do in Phoenix?"
"Vegas?"

After they drank another beer in a plastic Mexican tortilla cup, they left. The underwater tunnel they seemed to be trapped in exploded, and they felt free swimming to the top. Would they drown? Would they be lost at sea? Faster, "We got to get to Vegas, Akari. We must feel the desert breeze and inhale the strip fumes with our alcohol drenched nostrils. We have to hear subways and trains, screeches, see crutches, move the giant foundations of downtown burned-out hotel hangers, clogged drains, Plaza balconies with view of Golden Gate lights. We need to jump from the balcony and land safely because Akari, this will not last forever. This adventure will find us starting up a car in a suburban driveway and smiling to meet social requirements. Saying hi to passers we knew in college or in the restaurant business, on streets that we have outlived and outgrown. Please Akari, this isn't always." Taze lifted up a wine glass in New York New York café and proclaimed their innocence. "World, you have violated us. I, from The Watchtower and you from awful family expectations. But now we are!"

"Are what?" whispered Akari.
"Are what? We Are," replied Taze, "We are."

They entered the first hotel of their choice but after being in a car with Knob Creek, they didn't appear so

152

great. Instead, they looked slovenly disheveled with Brian Jonestown Massacre tee and short pleated denim skirt. They approached the counter surrounded by miles of chandeliers dancing above them. "A room, please any floor." The smug recent UNLV business school graduate looked at them and said, "No vacancy."

"But this hotel has seventeen hundred rooms, and it's an insignificant Sunday. What are you talking about?"
"No rooms, sorry."
"Listen, do you know who we are? I am the great artist Taze. I write novels. This is the author of *Severed Thighs*, the famous poetry book. Your rooms need us. We don't need them. Now get us a room."

"We're gonna collapse at an unknown destination tonight, and when we wake up, the sun will etch initials deep into our skin and we'll ask, why . . . why have these letters been branded permanently? And Akari, you'll say something to me. You'll cry, too."
"Taze, what . . . what will I say? What shape will my tears be? Will my cheeks shrink from salty dryness after the tears have stopped?"
"Eventually we'll be on some hair pin turn at twelve thousand feet. We'll be drunk. We'll be singing songs and taking corners at seventy-three miles per hour. The trees on each side of us will stumble, or I mean we'll stumble near trees."
"A canoe? Who cares?"

When she saw words in between the clouds, the car automatically grew wings, and she rolled the windows down. They inhaled the whiteness, and the car stopped, but they continued to ascend higher. Their surroundings grew dark, but nearing a star that sparkled, she smiled and off her teeth came a reflection that darted into his eyes. They both dozed off.

"Andrew Sound, nice to meet you." The man at the computer held out his thick hand and was hopeful for a hearty return from Taze. Taze shook.

"What's this place all about Andrew?"

"It's a thrift shop. I used to own it. Now I just work here." Akari looked at some used clothing. Taze spoke again, "I'll buy a shirt then. We are going to the Tom Waits show tonight."

Off of a dusty rack in the back, he pulled out a glowing purple shirt. It shined at the show.

After the show, they walked toward their auto hotel. Taze's phone rang. He saw an unrecognizable number. He showed Akari, "Do you recognize this number?"

"Oh shit! It's my sister!"

"You answer it then."

"I don't want to."

"Well, I'm not going to answer. Your family hates me. They think I stole your dad's car."

"See if she leaves a message."

She left a message. Taze and Akari sat on a curb. Each held a forty of Old English 800. They looked at the glow of the phone screen and listened to a shaky voice with a light Japanese accent.

"Taze, I need to talk to Akari now. It's serious. I can't leave a message to tell her. She needs to come home."

Akari grabbed the phone and returned the call. Taze walked away.

"It's Akari. What happened?"

"Akari, where have you been? I've been trying call for two days. You know how hard it was to get Taze's number."

"Sorry, I lost my phone, but what happened?"

The sound of crying begun on the other end.

"What happened?"
"It's mom and dad. They got into an accident."
"What happened?"
"They're   gone   Akari.   They're   gone."

Part 6- "Let's not be L7"
(Mid-2003)

Taze heard a startling knock on the steel apartment door. He looked through the smeared peep hole to see a stocky built man. He opened the door, and Horace smiled his characteristic smile, a smile with a fifty/fifty split of mischief and intellect. In his hands he held a small backpack and a VHS copy of *Fear and Loathing in Las Vegas*. Horace made the thousand-mile journey from Richmond, Virginia to El Paso, Texas to visit Taze and didn't even tell him.

Taze put the movie into the slot. The movie refused to play correctly. He lost the remote control years ago, and the movie needed some serious tracking. He needed to tap the tracking button quickly and repeatedly. Minus, minus, minus, etc. Eventually, the picture would have clear up, but Taze lost the remote.

Horace brought over some organic butter, organic popcorn, organic eggs, and organic grits for breakfast. Taze fiddled with the videocassette recorder and hoped for a miraculous recovery. He removed the top and saw what epitomized the previous complexity of a past technological world. He took one long look and heard a quick popping noise. He inspected it carefully. A fuse turned black, and the VCR lost power.

They drove to the large home improvement store to buy a fuse. Horace approached the counter and displayed the fuse in the air between his thumb and index finger. He hung the less than one-inch object, high.

"Where can we find this exact fuse?"

They found the fuse, and it cost $.39. Horace, owning a business, suggested that we steal it because it would cost the store less money than to process our credit card transaction. They paid anyway and replaced the fuse. The VCR still didn't work.

*　　*　　*

Horace demanded the repair.

"Can you fix this?" Horace asked with sincerity.
"What seems to be the problem?"
"We don't know. That's why you're our man!" Horace said with zeal.
"Let's have a look." The handyman looked at it and said, "The main circuit board is broken."
"Is that serious?"
"Hundred dollars to fix. You're better off buying a new one. Cost you more to fix it."
"Actually, can you repair it anyway?" Horace asked meekly.
"Buy yourself a new one."
"Can you repair it anyway?"
"All right then. Be ready in a week."

The twang in the handyman's voice melted like a steel guitar.

*　　*　　*

"Were you lonely?" Taze asked as he laid on the long puke green couch with the ceiling fan light in his eye.
"Absolutely!"
"Were you depressed?"
"I still am."
"Clinically, right?"
"Absolutely, no question."
"I see."
"When you spend time in a Jehovah's Witness household, you feel like you are never going to die, but then the moment comes when you realize that you are absolutely going to die. It comes as a thief in the night, unavoidable. It hits quick and hard, and there

157

you are standing in the middle of the Chihuahua desert naked and sad."

Enough.

I need to tell the truth. Wooly Bully is on the radio.

*   *   *

Horace slow cooked the bacon with precision and concern. He placed a cast iron pan, the diameter of the sun, on the smallest old fashion, three thick-coiled electric burner. The old stove took several minutes to heat up. Taze wondered how it affected those millions of families in the mid-1970's.

The organic grits told another story. The bacon cooked slowly.
"I haven't been regular," Horace stated as he paused looking forward and standing like a short order cook.

While the bacon slow cooked, Horace sat naked on the toilet with the door open. Taze walked over to him.
"Really Irregular?" Taze asked.
"I think I found a solution for my problem."
"You have?"
"Organic grits."
"What are grits?" Horace lived in Virginia for several years now and adapted to the local culture in this way almost exclusively. He learned how to make grits.
"It's just grain. It really helps me in the morning, more than coffee."

He got off the toilet and looked deeply into the bowl. With the exception of several slightly yellowish and extremely small rosary bead particles, it sat empty.

He cooked a delicious breakfast. Bacon, organic eggs, organic grits, wheat bread, and organic butter. Taze made some tea. They enjoyed themselves as the sun shone through the windowpane and an almost microscopic spider climbed its way up the wall painted white.

*   *   *

> "Matty told Hatty
> About a thing
> That she saw."

Taze's uncle was born around 1950. Oldies radio played during the car ride to the five Jehovah's Witness meetings a week. As a child, when Taze heard the searing melodies of Wooly Bully or even Louie Louie, he contemplated questions about the nature of existence, even at the age of four. The two major questions that concerned the existence of Wooly Bully: What is this? And why is this? Taze learned the "what" part at about 12, but he's been wrestling with the "why" part his entire life. When he arrived to the meeting, he sat and thought about Wooly Bully.

*   *   *

Taze and Horace grew up in a predominately Catholic neighborhood in Cleveland. They called the Watchtower meetings mass to their friends. They didn't attend mass. They attended the Kingdom Hall.

Everything centered around The Watchtower. Their families, friends, actions, records, TV, thoughts, pictures, picnics, water, air, memories, all dictated by The Watchtower. Horace's parents got baptized in 1976. Only Jehovah's Witnesses know the insanity of that decision. Horace heard the same Sam the Sham and the Pharaohs factoids on the sleepy Sunday morning drive to the Kingdom Hall. For twenty-two consecutive years, Taze and Horace attended meetings on Friday night, with the final one on December 31, 1999.

Taze's uncle got baptized in 1970 in order to gain minister status to dodge the Vietnam War. It didn't work. His aunt got baptized two years later.

When seated in that unreasonable front row looking at Jesus, Taze noticed in his book of Bible stories that Jesus did not hang from a cross, but rather, on a long straight wooden plank. The Jehovah's Witnesses teach that Jesus did not die on a cross, but on a stake instead.

In Taze's favorite hymn, the songwriters expressed the matter poetically with the touching couplet:

He died upon a tree
To set all mankind free

*   *   *

Taze ate lunch with a group of twelve people or so. They sat at an elongated table. The restaurant included a charge for gratuity for parties of more than 8 at a rate of 18%. Taze didn't say a word for fear that he may sound worldly or at least doubtful in the sense that he may say something intelligent concerning topics Jehovah's Witnesses never discuss and/or have never even heard about (e.g., Bakunin's- *God and the State*) and that might send the collective brain of the Witnesses into severe and sudden shock.

So, Taze chose not to speak. Some people would find it difficult and painful not to speak in a group so large. There must be somebody out of twelve who he could comfortably express some polite small talk. He didn't talk, and he found it satisfying and pleasant like a seventy-degree spring afternoon. They seem to have had fun with their conversations. They probably thought to themselves, "God, he's awfully shy, just sitting there, not saying a word."

*   *   *

Taze was born in 1977. Horace was born in 1975. They often shared memories of riding in the back seat of the red Chevette with the enormous older women in the congregation. Steel towns can be friendly but dirty. Greasy breakfasts went for usually no more than $.99 and that included coffee and overweight, gray-haired waitresses who delivered food quickly and with precision.

Several plates of hot food
at once
on one arm

where the thick residue

of home fries
attached itself
to the area
between the bicep
covered with fat

and
the forearm

with a faded tattoo.

Large bearded blue-collar men

waited

with excitement.

Taze and Horace frequently sat in this scene during field service coffee breaks.

Did they have a chance?

Dreaming of oil filters by eight, praying every day and night to Jehovah who provided the food, especially the $.99 breakfasts. Jehovah created the lard, the crunchy pancake, and the French toast. Dreams of Bethlehem Steel, beaches so polluted they banned eating the fish. Snow eight months straight, and the hope that the lake would freeze before February.

In third grade, Taze wore the same jeans almost every day of the school year. This didn't help to stop the bullying for being the only Jehovah's Witness in the class and one of only three in the entire school.

Horace sat next to Taze at meetings fascinated with the plastic clips that filled in the metal corners of the orange and yellow burlap chairs. He understood the giant urinal in the men's room and the small steel hook on the toilet door that slipped perfectly into the small steel hole attached to the doorframe, like consummating the marriage vow. Shades of powder blue, cheap wood, a fan so loud it drowned out the sound of urine hitting the porcelain curves of the stained bowl.

There they were in 2003 dancing to Wooly Bully. Not yet PIMO.

*   *   *

They left El Paso, Texas in Taze's Jeep Wrangler, ready for the junkyard, for a ride through the desert to a shanty shady town in Mexico called Palomas. A town so desperate and dusty, they just let people cross the border without a word or look. This was the town Pancho Villa crossed over from to take back the vast desert of what is now New Mexico aka "The Land of Enchantment."

They left at 6pm in the darkness of the early night. Helicopters flew overhead looking for what the local cowboys called "illegals," attempting to make the heroic dash to the factories and farms of the United States.

162

They entered the empty cantina. The sound of loud ranchero music blasted from the sound system. Cracked cement and broken tiles filled the place. Horace felt like dancing in this pleasure dome. He whirled and twirled his stocky body, arms and fingers, moving awkwardly and spinning. He wore tight fitting, side striped, blue athletic pants. Suddenly, an abuela ran in yelling, "We are not Indians!" Taze videotaped the incident, and abuela didn't appreciate it.

Just down the dusty, lawless street sat another cantina that outlawed cameras but allowed dancing. Horace danced to Wooly Bully. After it ended the song "Oh Sweet Pea" played on the sound system. They crossed the border, and the agent asked them questions, but Taze's thoughts of Sam the Sham distracted him.

If God exists, Sam the Sham must.

*   *   *

Sometimes Taze ate lonely with dust in the caterpillar toast and oatmeal in their fried chicken dreams. Sam the Sham would always be present with his glue and his towel hat. The sand would soil the inner tube of his nose, and pretend snot glowed.

*   *   *

Never had Taze longed for hope as on that day in the desert surrounded by tortillas. The mountains began to resemble statues, and the bridges over the Rio Grande held striking similarities to circus giraffes.

*   *   *

John Oates was one half of the eighties rock duo Hall and Oates. Generally, Daryl Hall received most of the fanfare. Together they produced such memorable hits as "Out of touch, Out of Time," "Adult Education," "Method of Modern Love," "One on One (I want to play that game tonight)," and, of course, the classic song dealing with marital infidelity, "Family Man

(Leave me the fuck alone)." Most critics praised their cover of the Righteous Brothers love anthem, "You've Lost that Lovin' Feeling." John Oates provided the haunting vocals in that lyrical tragedy of love lost and regained.

Peter Fonda was a musician in his own right, but his claim to fame (besides being Jane Fonda's brother), was as the freewheeling introspective motorcycling side kick of Dennis Hopper in the 1960s counterculture film *Easy Rider*. Fonda appeared in many other films and won a Golden Globe award for his role as the mysterious, yet courageous beekeeper in *Ulee's Gold*. One scene featured Fonda signaling to a gas station attendant with a raised arm after filling up his tank while speaking to the local sheriff.

In 1977, the two talented entertainers collaborated on the soundtrack of the biker film, "Outlaw Blues." John Oates penned the song for Capitol Records, while Peter Fonda provided the vocals. (FYI- Fonda sang a haunted house rendition of the Scotsman Donovan's "Catch the Wind").

*   *   *

Taze sensed sincerity in the compliments he received from other people about the taste of his homemade chili. He used beer, meat, and some peppers, onions, and canned ingredients. He knew anyone could make it. While he prepared the chili, he cut up a jalapeño and touched his already desert parched lips with his finger. He used Vaseline, but his chapped lips still burned. His butt crack chafed, as well. He listened to the music of The Stone Roses who covered Simon and Garfunkel with different lyrics, "Elizabeth my Dear" or as Simon and Garfunkel called it, "Parsley, Sage Rosemary, and Thyme," spices that Taze never used in his chili.

164

His lips burned up. He screamed. Horace couldn't hear him because he turned up Earth, Wind, and Fire's "That's the Way of the World" to maximum volume.

Horace always called it their song. To Taze, their song was "Wooly, Bully." Taze ran into the bathroom and washed off his lips. The chili smelled wonderful. It gave him a warm feeling. Horace ate some chili. He wouldn't turn the music down except to blow a fart and, because of his irregularity problem that the organic grits had yet to cure, his farts smelled like a satanic, putrid, horrific, toxic, stale post-industrial city or like Cleveland. It seemed only Taze held the power to smell them. Horace couldn't. Taze contemplated not serving Horace the chili. He served it anyway.

*   *   *

We took him to Niagara Falls. He lived in Malaysia and held a very lofty position at The Watchtower Branch. He resembled more robust Mahatma Gandhi. He didn't wear a robe and seemed well fed.

At the falls, he hesitated walking across the Rainbow Bridge to the Canadian side because he felt the Americans may not let him back in. Taze encouraged him to be risky. He took the plunge and approached the American border agent and politely asked, "Excuse me, sir, I (an Indian/English accent) wanted to go to Canada, but I'm not sure if I can come back to the U.S.?"

"Let me see your passport!"
"Thank you, sir."
"You can cross."

Rhada thanked the little balding white man with a slight nervous bow and stuttered his feet backwards, starting his walk over the Rainbow Bridge.

*   *   *

Horace burst into Taze's West Texas slum and shouted, screamed, yelled, and gestured with craziness, "I had a vision of pressure washing and restoring the exteriors of homes!" He spoke at length.

"I was mentally ill in San Diego. I called handy men to go with them on their jobs to help them free of charge. I wanted to learn. One man had me bash down a shed and demolish it. Why was a smart kid doing this? I called a guy named Dean, not a total redneck, but his voice went that way. He lived in a filthy apartment and was on the internet a lot trying to sell chemicals overseas. It was when the internet just got started. He had an ad in the OB Rag that said, 'handy man.' I called him."

"I met Dean about a block and a half from the ocean. I didn't know anything at the time, and nothing was working, but I felt like I was on the verge of something spiritual. Dean was really a nice guy, and he helped me. He taught me to pressure wash. I only wanted to work construction, and when I was 23, I felt like everything was there for the taking. Dean was discreet when asking me why I was doing this."

"I called *him*. He was a handy man, one of the lousiest professions in the world, but I thought it was the loftiest. We ate breakfast and then installed a water heater. I was in awe."

"It was amazing. He showed me how to clean off an old pipe with a wire brush. We were paid $80. I was so excited about the measly $80. He gave me $15. We went to this place for pot pies and installed an air conditioner in a house/day care service. Dean said that he rents tools. He doesn't buy them. I thought, "why not buy them?" He kept stressing the pressure washing. I didn't want to believe him. I wanted to clean carpets, install air conditioners, and mow lawns."

"Look at me now. I own one of the premier pressure washing companies in Richmond."

Horace went silent for a minute reflecting on something, perhaps an important detail. He looked up and started to talk to Taze again. "I lived with an overweight divorced limo driver. He had a beeper. The house we shared was filthy. He was a San Diego beach bum. I was from Cleveland, and I always cleaned up the place and left his apartment spotless. I was cooking a lot and eating a lot of burritos and sour cream and listening to a lot of 2Pac. A witness from a neighboring congregation who had a totally rebuilt leg hired me. He asked me to fix his pressure washer. I had no knowledge of how to. I saw the pressure washer and took it apart. I was full of grease. I didn't have any anti-depressants. His wife was in the house. She was really hot, actually. She told me I can use the shower. She was really sweet. I put my greasy clothes in the washing machine. She gave me a blue fuzzy robe. I was talking to her at the kitchen table. It was 3:30 pm. He came home and yelled at me furiously and kicked me out. He actually pushed me out the front door. Then, he told his elders who told my elders. It was a big mess. His wife wasn't even a witness, and the guy was inactive. He hadn't turned in time for two years."

*   *   *

"I'm shaking. My bodies rattling. Too much caffeine, sugar, I don't know, I'm just shaking. Maybe I'm nervous. Too much coffee, not enough 5-HTP or Nutropal or Valerian root, or Kava Kava or Xanax, no, not enough, yes, still shaking. I ate too much organic bran. My stomach hurts. I can't go to the toilet now. I'm indisposed at the moment. My entire digestive system hurts. Too much endive and romaine, too much organic bean burritos."

"I have to clean up my room, put clothes away, make the bed, do the laundry, vacuum (don't have a vacuum cleaner), do the dishes, open the windows, dust, open doors, hand wash the cast iron pan, make eggs again, store up some hard-boiled eggs, a banana sounds good, but oh my stomach. Maybe some music, what should I listen to, to stop shaking? I really had a bad dream that never ends. It's time to go to the meeting."

*   *   *

Douglas, Arizona housed a tiny clothing store that imports designer button down shirts from Milan, Italy. The shirts cost only $25.

Horace danced with joy. His arms contorted in an absolutely anti-rhythmic manner. His feet followed a basic disoriented pattern which changed to abstract circular digressions on the dusty and worn border town carpet. Horace is half Italian but lacks the "Tony Manero" genes necessary for good dancing in front of Latina sales associates. So, they giggled, and a smile appeared on Horace's face. They will never know he.

*   *   *

Taze searched tirelessly for a connection between his surrogate hero Sam the Sham and the pseudo-nerd Scottish rock duo "The Proclaimers." He realized, even before the search began, that he treaded in very deep waters. The possibility that these artists held a connection seemed slim. Of course, there existed the obvious commonalities of these entities, such as: they're both rockers, and they both had one major hit followed by a minor hit, but that wasn't enough. Taze needed a solid link in the figurative chain.

Sam the Sham was Mexican. The Proclaimers were Scottish. Sam the Sham sang whimsical tales of beasts with two horns and about mean-spirited wolves. The Proclaimers sang of the struggles and sacrifices on

168

love's path. Sam the Sham made his mark in the 60's, the Proclaimers in the 90's. So, he had a very difficult task, one that discouraged as well as motivated him. He began his search with energy.

First, he did the obvious. He searched the discographies and examined song titles. No match. But what he discovered ended his search for a link. On the CD entitled, "The Best of Sam the Sham and The Pharaohs," one song stuck out. The title? "Wanted, Dead or Alive." It clicked. He had been searching for the wrong link. His attempt to find a connection between Sam the Sham and The Proclaimers proved futile. He should have been seeking the conjoinment of Jonathan Francis Bongiovi and Richard Steven Sambora to Sam the Sham. Only his subconscious understood the Sambora/Sammudio connection, but more significantly, they both penned a song called, "Wanted Dead or Alive."

Although the songs differ in character (Sammudio's song is a silly old western tale while Sambora's song draws a somber picture of the mid to late 20th century literary "loner" riding his "steel horse"), they are exactly the same in title and length. So, to quote the irrepressible Jim Peterick of the band Survivor, "The search is over, you were with me all the while."

*   *   *

It was one of those nights. Horace was so angry and sad that he wanted to bash his head with a large cast iron pan. There is no Xanax or beer, and he didn't even have any cereal to eat. So, he laid down on the old, faded couch that was once part of somebody's perfect living room design but was now farted upon regularly by its fourth owner. He lived this night often and was about to finally fall asleep at 1am.

He just finished eating a $.33 frozen burrito, the kind that replaced Metamucil in his diet, when he decided to flip through the channels once more. As he flipped, he saw a Sheena Easton infomercial, an old boring b/w movie, college volleyball, a Latino standup comedian, reruns of Law and Order, Saved by the Bell, and the Corey Haim E True Hollywood Story. None of these programs interested him. But then on channel 71, there it was: C. Thomas Howell and Courtney Thorne Smith pool side in bathing wear.

Taze watched Horace from a distance. He wondered why Horace stopped on the channel with this film.

Horace felt compelled to look for a moment. Courtney Thorne Smith was about to dive into a large swimming pool occupied by *Soul Man* star, C. Thomas Howell. You could almost see his Pony Boy. She never made that dive because he managed to offend her somehow. Then, Bernie, from *Weekend at Bernie's I* and *II*, appeared in the movie. Horace continued to watch and Taze continued to watch Horace watch. Howell later befriended the guy with the beard and longhair from the steamy and sexy eighties courtroom series "L.A. Law." They formed an uneasy bond and became beach volleyball heroes. Courtney Thorne Smith, or as Horace later called her: C. Thorne Smith, reappears and finally falls for C. Thomas Howell after he wins an important volleyball match.

*   *   *

Taze earned about $30,000 a year to be insulted, yelled at, taken advantage of, overworked, underappreciated, crapped upon, and made to feel stupid. He fulfilled all the requirements for a sixth-grade teacher. He babysat kids, pleased parents, pleased the state, pleased the administrators, and even pleased the custodians.

People on the outside told him things like, "It's a noble profession, or it's a rewarding career." Some teachers complained about everything. Taze never did.

170

He only wanted to work, go home, and enjoy the summers off.

One day he stood in the hallway and heard his students make fun of his shoes, shoelaces, haircut, belt, tie, and socks . Students could say whatever they wanted to a teacher, but if a teacher said one mean thing to a student, the teacher breaks countless school district rules and laws. So, Taze kept his mouth shut.

The Principal walked up to him and said, "See me tomorrow during your conference period." Words Taze dreaded hearing. It could mean a parent called to complain or that somehow, he screwed up. He quickly thought about the possibilities of the meeting. "Why would she want to talk to me? There are so many things I did wrong, what could it be? Did I show too many movies in class? Did she discover that the third quarter grades I emailed in were an exact copy of the first quarter grades? Did she realize that all I do is hand out work while I sit at my computer or that my lesson plans are fiction? All teachers do that crap. If she busts me, I'm taking down the entire staff with me."

After two hours of emotional terror, he decided to quit. He said to her, "Whatever you're going to complain to me about is irrelevant because I quit!" He walked out. His legs shook. He left all of the useless school related crap in his classroom. He felt satisfied until he wondered to himself, "How am I going to earn money now?"

He rethought the situation and walked back to her office to beg for his job. She gave it back and only reprimanded him for "losing focus."

*   *   *

"If you work hard, you can accomplish anything!" Thus spoke Rudy Ruteger. Off of the success of the

171

movie "Rudy," based on his life story, Rudy Ruteger toured the country giving motivational speeches to thousands of bored high school students. Taze liked the movie, *Rudy*, because it had the kid from *The Goonies* in it, and it kind of inspired him.

Taze never found much inspiration as a young Jehovah's Witness. A working-class youngster from Cleveland, concerned mostly with smoking marijuana. The song "Yellow Submarine" inspired him the most at fifteen years old. He lived with a lot of poor people forced to live together in a rundown depressed steel town.

When they announced the visit of Rudy Ruteger excitement and energy filled the air like the black smoke from the 1970's, as if Bethlehem Steel returned. Signs posted, flyers passed out, announcements made by the principal. For once, the nerds on the student council did something right. It generated so much enthusiasm that the rumor that the hometown hero Ben Roethlisberger also planned to visit. Of course, this visit spread like unemployment through the area, and the dilapidated industrial buildings suddenly took on a pinkish crystalline glow.

The day before Rudy's arrival at Lincoln West High School, people feverishly cleaned it spotless and decorated it perfectly. A giant banner hung on the front, "Welcome Rudy Ruteger: You inspire us all!"

The moment finally arrived. Everyone in the school waited with anticipation for third period. The schedule read as follows:

Third period- Rudy's speech

Fourth period- a series of open questioning from the student body.

Fifth period- autographs followed by a raffle for a Notre Dame Football helmet and Jersey.

Sixth through eighth periods- A special airing of the Hollywood hit, *Rudy*.

Rudy stepped on the stage wearing a white tee shirt that read "GO FOR IT!" in big black letters. An insignia behind the phrase showed an airbrushed teenager flinging her fist in the air, not completely unlike a Black Panther Party fist. The microphone produced some howling feedback, and Rudy said, "Hello Cleveland! When I was 16 years old, I had a dream of playing football for Notre Dame, and I accomplished that dream."

"I put my mind to it and worked my tail off until I did it. I faced obstacles that seemed insurmountable. I faced setbacks every step of the way, but in the end, I did it. I accomplished my goals." The audience cheered vigorously.

"I grew up in a steel town just like you," he pointed. "When the steel plants moved away, our entire town was depressed. There were no jobs. People turned to crime to survive. The whole region was saddened. But you know what? I didn't sit around crying about it. I set a goal for myself, and I worked to accomplish it." Over the next 30 minutes, he continued with the same type of rhetoric with ambiguous and impractical advice.

And now, only a few years later, Taze thought about Rudy and that day and realized that he hadn't accomplished anything, and neither had Cleveland. Both were miserable and depressed and only a Rudy like miracle could save them.

*   *   *

They took the Jeep. Two rednecks. Taze could not understand what John Baxter of Baxter Auto Transport said. Baxter, with his very tan body and wilted white tank top, put the jeep on the truck.

The group of teens, who lived downstairs from Taze, must have thought, "God, that guy in the apartment upstairs just listens to music and paces around." The teens partied constantly. Streams of young people filed in and out and smoked weed and drank. Taze peeked into their apartment one time and saw that their garbage strewn place resembled the morning after a grand fiesta while his garbage strewn place looked like the disgusting bachelor pad of a dirty depraved soul.

Taze sat on the couch in the same spot repeatedly, over and over again. It started to fade like his hair. He learned new combing styles, new ways to move his forehead, new types of mousse and horse tail.

He flipped the couch cushions and found an exact replica of the faded spot on the other side.

*   *   *

Mitochondria nightmares.

*   *   *

The morning burst with cheerfulness. The sun smiled its second-grade coloring book smile. Horace rose up and jumped out of bed rising and shining, ogling at the sunny side up eggs. Fortunately enough, the birds sang a glad tune of spring preparations. The branches of the trees were welcoming arms of loved ones.

Horace stood at the six am stovetop. Taze got out of bed and when he walked into the kitchen, Horace smiled as wide and white as the linoleum under his thick bare feet. The nail on his big toe noticeably protruded longer than the rest, as if he trimmed and groomed the other four toes regularly but ignored the big one. Even the hair on his big toe grew wild like the poppy plants on Mount Franklin. Taze stood behind him and spoke trying hard to deflect the impressions made by his burgundy boxer briefs with yellow waistband. Intimidated, he asked, "Why are you so cheery?"

He turned his neck sideways while his body remained straight, facing his eggs. The sideward arch looked strained, but his smile remained. "I'm singing with the birds today, my friend. I'm singing with the birds."

One egg hung on the edge of the spatula for a moment and slid onto the dish with only a subtle turn of the wrist. "My grandmother always used olive oil to make her eggs." He smiled. It tasted damn good. Just the way Taze liked an egg: lightly salted and daintily prepared.

*   *   *

Taze lived in Ft. Lauderdale at the time and imagined what the sun must look like as he hid out in the tiny apartment that cost $1300/month. On a perfect winter day, the internet provided the startling news that Air Supply, the 80's pop/rock ballad band, announced two shows in early February in Orillia, Ontario, Canada. Since Taze grew up in Cleveland. He could drive to Orillia. He called Denny, who agreed to go with him. He still lived in Cleveland, but he agreed to meet in Buffalo, NY.

Taze quickly bought the plane tickets and the Air Supply tickets. Horace decided to make the trip down to Ft. Lauderdale from Richmond. From Ft. Lauderdale, Horace and Taze flew to N.Y.C. Terrible winter storms brewed in Buffalo. They shut down all the bridges to Canada except one, The Peace Bridge. Their original flight out of N.Y.C. was cancelled. The concert started at 9pm. The flight arrived in Buffalo at 6pm. Denny picked them up, but time was tight.

Life moved ahead at regular speed in Orillia, no storm could stop Air Supply from taking the stage. Whether they made it on time or not, 80's rock heroes, Air Supply, would play, and play they did.

Taze, Horace, and Denny crossed the border, bought some duty-free beer, drank a little and drove very fast. They hit a bad snowstorm in Barrie, Ontario, Neil Young's birthplace. Horace peed on the side of the Queen Elizabeth Expressway. The wind floated his urine and almost crystallized it as it blew away.

They arrived at the Indian Casino venue a little late and missed the first two songs. Horace faced some anxiety while in the will call line. Chinese people flooded the venue, and Taze realized Chinese people love Air Supply. A large sign promoted the band Credence Clearwater Revisited. He always thought the name was Revival.

He saw Graham Russell Hitchcock.

They sat very high up in the arena. Russell Hitchcock (the short guy with the afro) thanked the fans in the high seats for attending despite the "lack of oxygen up there." Horace leaped up and shouted, so that the entire crowd could hear, "You're our Air Supply!"

After the show, they noticed people lined up for pictures and autographs. From up close Russell Hitchcock stood about 6 feet tall. He only looked short because his partner Graham Russell stood close to Yao Ming's height. Taze shook their hands, and the two rock stars gave them autographs.

Air Supply maintained a high level of charm and class in their roles as modern-day minstrels who sang about love with heavy homoerotic overtones.

Denny shook Hitchcock's hand again and as he walked away Hitchcock mentioned in a somewhat meek operatic voice, "You look like Tim Robbins, but you're a lot nicer."

Taze sat in West Texas and recalled the whole incident.

*　　*　　*

There were times when major moral and ethical decisions had to be made. One example for Taze, "Should I smoke marijuana or not?" When questions like this arose, he asked himself, "What would Sam the Sham do in this situation?"

*　　*　　*

Taze's teapot burnt to a crisp on the bottom. He once used it to iron a shirt, but now, it gave off a rancid odor. Chamomile tea helped him to fall asleep. It relaxed him. He combined half & half, water, organic whole milk, sugar, and three tea bags in a big jug. He let it chill in the fridge. He forgot about it for a week. Actually, he looked at it and decided not to drink about 100 times or at least 8 or 9 times a day. Finally, he took a sip.

Even if he decayed inside, the flavor of the chamomile tea provided something he could depend on. Even if he wore the same socks three straight days, he could still enjoy the tea with a semi-clean conscience.

Then, Horace knocked on the door.

*　　*　　*

Taze thought he understood things. He drove his car fast. He got angry at individuals for flimsy, suspect reasons. He cursed frequently. He cared enough to practice mainstream ways of manifesting negative character traits, but as the dust piled up on his dining room table, he gradually changed.

177

Thick caked layers required Windex and all-purpose cleaner, a complete washing. This act of tidiness served a quick temporary purpose. The important question: "Did cleaning the table have any meaning beyond him and his apartment?" And the even larger question: "Did life have any meaning?"

Later he saw a large desert bug on the white wall in his bedroom, a rather intimidating insect. He left it alone thinking, "Well . . . if I didn't see it than it was never there. So, why not just let it hide itself? Most people will immediately kill the bug or trap it and throw it outside." Taze realized that the bug out of his sight meant no bug at all, or it ceased to exist, or maybe it never existed at all.

Taze let it live. After one day it only moved slightly to another spot on the same wall. Two days later he didn't see it anywhere, but on that same day, as he washed his hands in the bathroom, he saw it again on the white bathroom wall. He ignored it again. He took a shower, and when he finished, he reached for the towel he used four days that week (not consecutive), and, shockingly, the bug appeared on the towel. That drove Taze to action. He killed it. The song that played on the stereo as he killed it: "That's the Way of the World" by Earth, Wind, and Fire.

*   *   *

"Wake Up!" shouted Horace.

Taze didn't know if he meant it in some sort of philosophical sense. Horace's stratagem proved controversial. He dressed in burgundy athletic (plastic) pants with two yellow stripes that ran down the sides and also circled the waistband. No shirt, a cd player in hand, new tennis shoes, bright, and white, unshaven chin, flaring nostrils, and of course, a giant white smile that said, "Let's go!"

"Let's walk a mile or two," he belched.

"Are you totally sure, Horace?"

"It may look a certain way, but who cares! All that Watchtower fear of homosexuals and transgenders . . . . you need to get rid of that. Get it out of your mind." Then he asked a profound question: "Why can't two adult males walk side by side in a residential neighborhood without the fear of being perceived as homosexual partners? Like I said, Taze, let go of the fear." Horace's face contorted in what looked like pain as he finished the sentence.

"You're right man. Who cares! People around here don't care. It's all in our JW heads."

Then Horace looked at Taze, touched his shoulder, and like a brother, said, "Let's walk. Shall we?"

"Okay," Taze chuckled, "but you have to make me some organic eggs when we get back."

They left the upstairs apartment and said hello to the ambiguously drunk neighbor across the hall. Although Taze never got his name, he felt his aura. He was a bald, tall, skinny white man with a thick brown mustache. He drove a rundown Nissan RX7, a sporty red one. Every once and a while, Taze looked into his apartment for a split second to the sight of at least a dozen empty Relska Vodka bottles strewn on the floor.

The neighbor saw Taze and Horace at the bottom of the stairs. What did he think when Horace had his hand on Taze's shoulder while they pleasantly discussed organic eggs? Just two months earlier, Taze lived with a beautiful young Jehovah's Witness spouse. Now, she lived in Florida, and Horace looked like her replacement. What did the neighbor think of this sudden transition? What did he think of the varieties of aromas that floated out the window from Horace's elaborate breakfasts? What did he think of

179

the Earth, Wind, and Fire music coming from the spare bedroom window?

They politely said hello and began their walk. Horace walked at a very brisk pace and flailed his arms as he listened to his cd player. He didn't even talk to Taze. As they walked, they passed a church. A young pastor stood in front with a snow cone machine to his left. Horace stopped at the church and approach the young pastor.

"Snow cones!"
"Yes, snow cones. Would you two gentlemen like one?"
"We'd love one."
"Okay, I have coconut, grape, cherry, lemon, and blueberry, or I can do rainbow."
"I'll take the rainbow!" exclaimed Horace.

Taze chose the coconut.

"So, where you fellas from?" asked the young pastor.
"We're from Cleveland. My friend Taze moved to El Paso a couple of months ago."
"Taze. I like that name," said the young pastor.
Horace intervened, "What kind of church is this?"
"Non-denominational. Everyone is welcome. None are rejected. Do you go to church?"
"Well, we're Jehovah's Witnesses." Horace paused and then spoke, "Well, kind of."
"What do you mean kind of?"
"We were raised in the religion, but we have our doubts." Horace nibbled the edge of the rainbow snow cone with his two front teeth.
"I can understand why you two fellas have your doubts. In this church right here," the young pastor pointed at the church, "we accept everybody, and I mean *everybody*."
Taze licked the top of his coconut snow cone.

Horace cooked bacon countless times. On his second visit to West Texas, he felt it a necessity to review the proper procedures in bacon cooking. Horace and Taze hiked to the supermarket on a cool and mellow desert night. Horace always carried his "strap-on" miner's light which proved to be a "lamp to their feet and a light to their roadway."

Horace chose the bacon. He told Taze that in West Texas he must be leery of the cured bacon strips laced with fat. They bought the uncured variety.

Upon returning to the apartment, Horace reached for the largest cast iron pan Taze owned, the only one Taze owned, which Horace gifted him a year earlier. He turned the temperature of the smallest coiled stove burner to two, put the pan on it, and, with care and delicacy, placed five strips of uncured bacon neatly on the pan.

"So, how long does it take to cook?" Taze innocently asked with the expression of a newborn fawn.
"About an hour. You have to slow cook it."
"Why?"
"For maximum enjoyment."
Taze asked no further questions. To kill some time, they sat out on the balcony and sipped some Jim Beam Black whisky and talked. They talked of time and persons past.

The bacon took almost twenty minutes longer than expected. Horace served it, and Taze ate it.

*   *   *

The toilet paper roll ran out of paper. Taze thought the double rolls lasted forever. A thousand sheets, how did he possibly go through that many? How long did it take? He had one roll left. He quickly replaced the empty roll with a full roll. The small bathroom size

181

garbage can sat full, not even enough room for the cardboard cylinder. Two chores suddenly arose.

Taze flushed the toilet (an accomplishment, considering the context of the flush) and entered the shower. Clean boxers and a two-day used towel sat on the counter. The water ran, and he started to wash. Dried crevices filled the skinny and flat soap. Adding water smoothed the texture a bit. Taze eventually lathered and rubbed under his armpits. The little skinny soap slipped out of his hands to the shower floor. When it landed, it split into two pieces, one of which sailed down the drain and the other too small to use. Taze could have temporarily stopped his shower to reach under the sink and grab a new bar of soap. "That can wait until tomorrow," he reasoned.

Taze shampooed. That went well. He secured his still damp towel. It rested upon two coffee mugs. One with a dried brown crust at the bottom. The other will have a dried brown crust by tomorrow. He dried himself off and got out of the shower and started to shave. His electric razor cut countless short black hairs.

Taze also used a straight disposable razor for his chin and neck. He resurrected one with hot water and tapped it against the sink to remove more black hair from the last shave, over a week ago. The razor could have been discarded, but he preserved it on the counter because he wasn't ready to dump the garbage yet. The hand soap dispenser was empty. The mirror filled with water spots. The rugs were always a little wet. A dark Saturn ring lived in the toilet where the water stopped, and the naked porcelain began. He ran out of q-tips. His deodorant, caked with underarm hairs, spun to the top. The underarm hair so closely resembled pubic hairs, that if one cared enough, he could have accused Taze of caking the area above his dick.

Finally, for fun, Taze winked, took the empty toilet paper roll and looked through it as if it were a telescope.

*   *   *

Tazed planned his escape from West Texas. The hyper-conservative local elders at his congregation acted much different than the more liberal elders of south Florida. Taze barely attended meetings, and the elders snooped incessantly to find some wrongdoing. They sometimes sat parked outside his apartment waiting to see if a woman left. Upon the sight of Horace taking out the garbage in his burgundy boxer briefs, the elders called Taze.

"Hello, Brother Felix."

"Hello, Brother Dander."

"You know . . . we have to ask these questions."

"Yeah. Yeah. I know."

"We received a report from Sister Dangle that your wife moved back to south Florida and that there's now a man living with you."

"Well, no. He's not living with me. He's a witness, too. He's an old friend. And yes, my wife did move back to south Florida. I had to stay here because of a work contract."

"Is everything okay between you and your wife?"

"Yes. She was just homesick. That's all."

"You know I have to ask, but Sister Dangle said that she saw your friend walking around in his underwear and listening to . . . to use her words 'suggestive music.'"

"I must have been at work."

"It was around dinner time, and your car was there."

"I don't know. I don't know. What are you implying?"

"Do you have time for a scripture?"

"I'm sorry Brother Dander. I have to go. I have some food on the stove. I'll call you back later."

* * *

The last weeks in West Texas brought with it several hardships. Auto shippers picked up Taze's vehicle to transport to Florida, which forced Taze to ride his bike or walk as transportation.

To get to work, Taze accepted a ride from Juan, a 27-year-old Mexican national. He drove an old beat to hell Chevy Blazer. On the 25-mile ride to work he blasted Narco Corridos.

"Are you hype today?" he'd say. Taze would stare at him and quietly, respond, "Yes." He wasn't really hype.

"One time a white dude asked me if I play golf. You know what I said? Listen up. You know what I said."

"What did you say, Juan?"

"Listen up. This is what I told the white cat. I said I only play working class sports like basketball."

"Oh!"

"'Tiendes? you see instead of labeling something as poor or lower class, I always use the term working class because it denotes class consciousness. We need to get that idea into people's heads, class consciousness!"

"Okay, class consciousness."

"When the masses start recognizing class consciousness, then we can change the socio-economic structure of our repressive elitist institutions!"

"Good," I replied.

"I'm red!" He proclaimed.

"Good, good."

"That's why I teach social studies. We Mexicans are a repressed peoples living in conquered territory."

"Yes."

"Class consciousness."

"Yes."

184

Taze never wanted to disrupt Juan's enthusiasm by interjecting his feelings about the meaninglessness of life. Instead, he shared with him his hatred for the rich and his contempt for golf.

*   *   *

He went to work without underwear because he didn't do the laundry. He hadn't dusted any furniture in weeks. The sink filled with dirty dishes, which featured a yellow concrete liquid of unfinished sunny side up organic eggs. The front edge of the toilet seat stained with sticky urine as well as the floor tiles just below it. A clear pattern emerged. A pattern that depicted the consistency of the location of the stray urine drops. Taze bet that an expert in forensics could figure out his height, weight, diet, and every other vital stat through an examination of this distinct circle of stickiness. He avoided peeing sockless. He felt the crusty gluelike substance on his toes. He wore slippers. He kept them at the entrance of the bathroom and entered it like he entered a mystical Asian shrine.

Actually, he gave up on shoelaces altogether because of the time and difficulty involved to lace. Lifting up the toilet seat revealed some black stains. The neighbors saw him walk to his mailbox and stared. He imagined they thought, "What is that?"

*   *   *

The lower he went the more he dwelled upon Cleveland, OH and some things others could never understand. He attended the Kingdom Hall almost every day. He heard fifteen times a week, that before he turned twenty years old, that he'd witness the end of the worldly system of things. "Birthday" stood out as a dirty word in those circles because Jehovah's Witnesses don't celebrate them. They don't celebrate any holidays.

He sat in the Kingdom Hall as a child and thought, "Armageddon could happen right now. Am I going to die?" The building, as well as the people in it, needed major remodeling. Orange and yellow made up the main color scheme with elaborate triangle designs on the walls and behind the stage podium displayed a giant forested wallpapered scene. Real trees, not a painting, real trees for Taze to stare at while he sat in a frightened and bored stupor.

He thought, "If Armageddon comes right now, maybe Jehovah will make that giant forest wallpaper real, and we can run into the woods." Horace sat there, too. His parents believed the same stuff. They sat together in a strangely decorated building where people came to discuss the end of the wicked world just minutes from abandoned and shut down factory buildings.

Cleveland suffered through a real city-wide feeling of depression. Taze befriended a 36-year-old, 6-foot 10-inch Indian ministerial servant. He resembled the chief from *One Flew Over the Cookoo's Nest*. He wore his hair longer than the other servants in the congregation. His clothes consisted of mostly leisure suits and cheaply built sport coats. He drove truck. His listened to The Beach Boys.

The religion required meeting together on the coldest of Cleveland mornings to drive to decaying impoverished neighborhoods to hand out religious magazines. Taze always wanted to partner up with Brother Ponytail for two reasons. Brother Ponytail didn't care, and he'd take Taze out to eat breakfast.

It always went like this:

"So, why are you in this religion, Brother Ponytail?"
"I got involved to get out of Vietnam. If you were considered a minister, you didn't have to go. All I had

to do was work really hard in the church, and I'd get an exemption."

"Did it work?"

"I'm still alive, aren't I?" He was always cheerful when he said this.

Taze always replied, "Yes, you are!"

The waitress walked over, and Brother Ponytail flirted.

*   *   *

Mental stability eluded Taze enough without forcing himself to incessantly watch the movie *Ulee's Gold*. He rigged up his VCR to play the movie constantly in his bedroom on the thirteen-inch television set. So, no matter when or what time he walked into the room, *Ulee's Gold* played. At first, he'd just see the movie playing and go about his business. Whether he got dressed, danced about, or searched for clean socks in the giant pile of his wrinkled clothes, the movie played on with the sound at full volume.

He gave up sleeping in the bedroom when the bed became so cluttered with miscellaneous stuff that he couldn't fit on it. Since the apartment was small, he always heard the dialogue.

The same lines over and over again.

The same scenes over and over again.

The part where Peter Fonda gets gas for his car, over and over again.

The tale of the confused beekeeper, over and over again.

He began to log what scenes played at specific times of the day. For example, 6:37pm, 7:45 pm, 8:17pm, and 1:15 am. He searched for patterns, mathematical and otherwise. He dreamt about the movie almost every night and received flashbacks throughout the day. He quoted it to other people, unconsciously. He recommended it to strangers like attendants at gas stations, Arby's managers, random ranchers, vaqueros, rancheros, barmaids, etc. He finally confided in one particular person about his *Ulee's Gold* bedroom. He responded by saying "Man, I saw *Ulee's Gold*. You sure as hell have a high tolerance for boredom."

*   *   *

Horace wanted to grow a beard. He had the ability, but The Watchtower did not allow beards. Upward mobility within the religion proved impossible with a beard. His parents took it so seriously that they outlawed him from growing facial hair. They bought him razors and shaving gel and practically waited outside the bathroom door to "make sure of all things."

He felt he possessed a winning argument in the issue. He said, "Dad, the founders of this religion all had long scraggly beards."
"That's true son."
"The apostles all had beards."
"Yes, indeed."
"Jesus had a beard."
"Exactly."
"So, I should be allowed to grow a beard."
"No."

*   *   *

Taze paced again and again. He paced and listened to Earth, Wind, and Fire's "That's the Way of the World."

Day after day he saw an empty parking lot and neighbors moving out. He stared at the colorful distance of the West Texas sunset. He had a perfect view facing west. He imagined looking straight to California and that the beach sat just under his view, just far enough away in the distance where he couldn't see it. The oranges, yellows, and the purples of the setting sun, all in view. His brain set with it.

*   *   *

At about 10pm, on very hot and dry El Paso night, hunger pains hit Taze. His supply of food dwindled to nothing, and 1000 miles away, his car sat parked in a condominium lot. Horace decided not to return to El Paso for another visit.

It began on that night of severe hunger. He walked about one-half mile to a gas station and bought two burritos, and two king cans of Busch beer. He wanted to start fresh in south Florida, so he gave away his furniture. On the floor of his empty apartment, he indulged in his food and drink purchases. He shoved the loathsome food and drink down his throat, like a child swilling cough syrup.

The nausea began moments later. Eventually, he slept. He woke up and brewed a cup of coffee. He thought, "Why not make this a healthy day by taking a bike ride?" It felt like he hadn't been out of the gloom of the apartment for weeks.

Work
Apartment
Work
Apartment
Work
Apartment

The sun shone. He felt almost human. His bike tires deflated. He tried not to worry about it. He walked the bike to the burrito gas station. He had $.25. Upon his arrival, he noticed the air machine still dispensing air. He pumped up his bike tires.
Last night's burrito started to take hold after he rode for a few minutes. He arrived back at his apartment and raced inside. He ran to the kitchen, poured coffee and in one motion, pulled down his pants and sat on the toilet. He placed his coffee on the tiled floor next

189

to the toilet. In his haste, he neglected to shut the bathroom door, and, at just the right angle, a random passerby could see in through the patio door. He stood up, hunched over a bit and shut the door for more privacy. When he did, he noticed one delicate, silent, crystalline tear drop of urine fall straight down like a nuclear bomb out of his penis. It traveled in a perfectly straight line and landed with a tiny splash into his coffee.

He sat back down on the toilet. He suddenly had a decision to make, and he knew he'd be sitting there for another five minutes. He loved to drink coffee on the toilet. He gazed at the coffee, which hadn't changed in color or consistency. He looked at the ceiling lights and the shower curtain while he ran his fingers through his hair. He looked side to side in wonder. He gazed at the coffee again. He noticed two pubic hairs laying elegantly on the tile next to the coffee mug. "Did they fall with the droplet?" he asked himself.

He drank the coffee.

*　　*　　*

Horace called Taze. Tazed watched *Ulee's Gold* while he ate Raman Noodles from the Styrofoam cup.

"Hello"
"I'm listening to . . ."
Taze interrupted Horace, "Horace, it's you!"
He ignored Taze words and continued, "I'm listening to Earth, Wind, and Fire."
"You sound content. Why?"
"Valerian Root, man." ("Shut up," he yelled at his dog.)
"Yeah, I like the stuff. I should buy a bottle."
"All natural. If I could only take a dump, things would be perfect."
"That would make things perfect? Have you taken anything else?"

"5-HTP, Nutropel, Kava Kava."

"That's quite a cocktail of natural drugs."

"I ate an organic brownie, some alfalfa, two bowls of raisin bran. I've been naked on the toilet for two hours imagining a bowel movement."

"Calm down. Drift away, Horace. Open up your mind and your bowel."

"I drank too much chamomile."

"Is that possible?" said Taze as he watched Peter Fonda pump some gas into his car while talking to the local sheriff.

"Remember the other night?"

"You mean Gregorson?"

"Yes, Gregorson."

"It made me kind of scared."

"It was spooky. It was really scary. I had a tough time sleeping."

*   *   *

The night before Horace returned to Richmond, him and Taze found some excerpts of Ray Franz's book *Crisis of Conscience* on the 2003 version of the internet (Web 1.5). The clock read well past midnight. Both finally opened up about their major doubts about The Watchtower. Both found it a huge relief to be able to speak to each other. This led them to the internet and C of C.

Despite their young ages, both remembered the major controversies that older ones gossiped about in the early 1980s. Things like private bible studies outside of the Kingdom Hall and the official literature of The Watchtower. Both remembered intensely graphic material about Armageddon, its violence, and its nearness in time. Both heard the gossip about the big apostasy at Bethel and the mass expulsions and witch hunts of brothers and sisters all over the United States.

191

They used the CD-ROM version of the Watchtower library and looked up the word "apostate."

"I can't believe this Horace! The word "Apostate" was barely used in the Watchtower or Awake before the early 1980s! That's incredible!"
"Holy shit! I know."
"So, what does that mean?"
"It means that apostasy wasn't really a thing until Ray Franz. It means that maybe people could leave the religion without shunning, until Ray Franz."
"It sounds like it. It sounds like you could disassociate without being shunned, until Ray Franz."

This moment shook Taze. He walked into his kitchen stunned. He felt so nervous reading this information. He didn't know how to react.

"Taze! Come in here!"
"Look! Look! Ray Franz was disfellowshipped for sharing a meal with his disassociated friend, Gregorson. The Watchtower created this rule because of Ray Franz!"

Horace searched for Gregorson's phone number and found a possible relative in Alabama. He called. The phone rang twice and a man that sounded middle-aged answered:

"Hello."
"Gregorson," said Horace.
"Who is this?"
"We know about your father or uncle or grandfather and Ray Franz. We read about it."
The man on the other end of the phone politely responded in a nervous tone, "It's really late. Yeah. We can talk about it later, but it's really late."

Horace continued, "It's terrible what they did. It's . . .
terrible!"

The man interrupted, "I know. It's late. I can't really
talk right now," and hung up the phone.

"It was him! It was Gregorson!"

"It's over, man. It's over. I can't do it anymore. No
more meetings. No more. I can't do it."

"Me neither. It's too much. I'm finished."

*   *   *

Horace sent Taze a check for twenty-five dollars. Taze
could bike to two branches of his bank. Fortunately,
his bank opened for four hours on Saturdays.

Taze could bike uphill, but closer, or on a flat road
over the state lone into New Mexico. He decided on
the flat burn over the state line into New Mexico. Late
May in the desert offered challenges, such as intense
dry heat, blaring sunshine, and scorpions on the side of
the road. He bicycled and bicycled the "red baron" (a
$59 Kmart Huffy) laboriously on the soft shoulder of
the cactus desert back road. His baseball cap kept the
sun out. The ten-year-old Toronto Maple Leafs tee
shirt hid sweaty thick armpit sweat. He crossed the
Rio Grande and entered the "Land of Enchantment."

His thirst bit hard. He needed some water or a sugary
sports drink. A crowded gas station sat across the
street from the bank. He parked the "red baron" and
entered. He found a 16oz plastic bottle of spring water
and approached the large woman behind the counter.
She rang it up, $.86. He handed her his credit card.
This confused her. She asked for ID. Taze showed her
his Florida driver's license. She said she couldn't
accept it because it was out of state. His thirst became
painful. Although she seemed confident in her
assertion, she asked the manager. He decided it was
okay and ran the credit card.

Meanwhile, heat exhaustion set in. He had no spit to speak of, and the bank closed in ten minutes. He guzzled down the water and jumped back on the "red baron" and rode across the street to the bank. They locked the front entrance. Taze saw several cars in the drive through.

Lanes one and three had three cars each while lane two had only one car. Taze used his common sense and chose lane two. He figured that it would take longer to service three cars than to service one car. He waited ten minutes. Cars almost seemed to pass right by the long tube on both sides of him, as if they had no wait time at all. Beautiful cars with beautiful people seemed to enjoy the weirdo on his bike in the middle lane. The teller laughed a little at Taze and warned him of the extreme danger involved in riding a bike through a bank drive through.

*   *   *

After Taze arrived home from work, he sat on his patio in the same clothes he wore every day. He called them his "after work clothes." Although he held a professional job as a public-school teacher, his work clothes and after work clothes took on a depraved resemblance to each other. His students described his clothes as wrinkled, soiled, smelly, and stained amidst more profane adjectives.

So, he sat on the patio when a stocky built teen walked underneath and yelled something about drinking a beer downstairs. Taze felt terror at the prospect of social interaction, especially with young worldly people. Taze yelled down, "No. I have my own beer, but thanks!"

About fifteen minutes later the same teen asked him again. This time Taze built up the courage to answer "YES!" He headed downstairs to a place that he heard through thin floors. It sounded like fun, partying, people, association, jokes, music, and tv. All the things

The Watchtower warned him about in the "Young People Ask" articles. The apartment below took on a mythical vision in Taze's imagination. Possibly a large flat screen television, a loud booming stereo, a full bar with top shelf liquor and stools, modern and trendy furniture, black ribbed turtlenecks, Aldo leather shoes, wine glasses, house beats, tofu, fondue, "YES!"

Taze walked downstairs and entered. Three guys in their late teens sat comfortably, one on a beanbag chair and two on Taze's old sofa. The apartment held a backwoods ambiance of depravity. Ashtrays, empty beer cans, wrappers, all sorts of trash strewn about.

Jared, Billy, and Jason sat there, smoking and drinking. Taze grabbed the beer they promised, Piel's Light from a thirty pack. The three guys wore cowboy boots, tank tops, and tattoos. They shouted over one another in conversation. They all believed strongly in Jesus.

Taze thought, "So, this is what The Watchtower was so worried about?"

*   *   *

The phone rang. It was Horace.

"Horace!" Taze screamed, "How's Richmond?"
"The locals are closing in on me. They've got me."
"What happened?" Taze asked him while he sat on the toilet eating an apple.
"Dog at large! Jail time!"
"What's dog at large?"
"Some new suburban law."

Taze understood and took the last bite of the apple. He placed the core near the sink.

"Listen, my dog got loose two times, and I got a warning from a cop. Then he got loose again, and I got a ticket for dog at large. I tried to pay the ticket when the cop gave it to me, but he said I have to go to court. I forgot to go to court and missed the date."

"Oh my god, you missed the court date!"

"Yeah, I know. So, they haven't issued a warrant for my arrest yet, but when they do, I have to turn myself in, spend a day in jail, get a new court date, go to court, and pay a fine."

"But isn't there major drug trafficking in your apartment complex?"

"I have to go to bed."

Horace hung up.

*   *   *

Taze woke up late the next morning and rushed through the obligatory morning coffee, morning excrement, and shower. He brushed his teeth, and, for about the tenth time, he knocked his toothbrush off the counter and into the extremely small palm tree decorated garbage can. Every time it happened, he thought to myself, "I couldn't do that if I tried."

He quickly noticed the brown apple core. Juan honked out front, and he ran down the stairs, but didn't see Juan's beat up Blazer.

It was Sunday, not Monday.

"Should I go to the Kingdom Hall?"

*   *   *

He walked to J.P.'s diner, a Mexican restaurant for some chile rellenos with some rice and beans and purchased a "King Can" of Busch beer on the way back. After he drank the beer, a noise bubbled in his stomach. When he first arrived in West Texas, he could handle eating a large plate of Mexican food topped with cheap beer, but he couldn't anymore. He lost it.

He ran back to his apartment and into the bathroom, sat on the toilet, and unloaded a dangerous mix. He felt relieved for a second and looked around. He did not see the apple core.

"I must have thrown it out and forgot about it," he thought.

Without a second thought he wiped and almost flushed. Suddenly, he stopped and stared deep into the bloody toilet mix as it moved like a slow flowing everglade. He gazed, stretching and straining his eyes below the mangled toilet paper, and he saw it. He saw the apple core beneath the waste, perfectly wedged in the hole at the bottom. It looked like a natural fit.

He had two options. Flush or reach his hand in and remove it. Before he made any decision, he wondered how the core got there, but he couldn't come up with an answer.

He decided to play it safe and reach in to take out the apple core with his raw naked hand. The phone rang, which offered a momentary reprieve. He answered.

"Dog at Large!"

He hung up the phone and ran back to the toilet and without a thought, he flushed. Only a second later he realized he made the wrong decision. The toilet water spun upward. The water level rose to the top along with everything else. "Please don't overflow!"

Taze thought of praying to Jehovah God. The phone rang again. He ignored it and watched the water stop at the top of the bowl. The water level could not have risen any higher. Taze thought to myself, "If I had peed even one more drop earlier, the result *would* have been a disastrous overflow."

Maybe Jehovah already intervened.

He closed the lid and left. It was at that point he fully appreciated having two bathrooms. Horace called again.

"Hello," Taze answered.
"Hey man! Are you okay?"
"Horace," Taze paused, "I think I'm going to be alright. Yes, Horace. I think I'm going to be alright."

As he said this to Horace, he smiled and shook his head up and down.

He repeated one last time, "I think everything's going to be alright."

*   *   *

Taze concocted tea combinations to create new drinks. He listened to "That's the Way of the World" by Earth, Wind, and Fire almost exclusively. Questions conquered his brain. "Would Horace rescue me? Will he knock on the door and save me? Would I survive seven more hellish workdays with children who hate me? How could I? Could I load all my stuff onto a truck alone? Could I clean this place up and get my security deposit? Florida, only a few days, and I'd be there."

He wanted to sleep through the next week and a half, but he knew he couldn't. He had to teach kids and prepare to move.

*   *   *

"Dad? Why can't I celebrate birthdays?"
"Because John the Baptizer was executed on a birthday celebration."
"Dad? Why can't I date the girl from school?"
"Because you can only date after the 'bloom of youth.' Paul says it in the bible."
"Dad? Is the end of the world coming soon?"

"Absolutely! According to bible prophecy we are living in the 'last days' son. It's right around the corner."

Horace should never have been 27 years old.

*   *   *

"Mister, Don't you ever iron your pants?"

Taze handed out assignments and sat behind his desk daydreaming. He only acknowledged the students to tell them to stop talking. His facade as a teacher thinned. His energy and motivation waned So, he showed them cartoons and let them work in groups. Anything to survive the day and go home.

He developed an idea for a group project. It allowed him sit back and do nothing while the students screamed, yelled, and beat each other up. He brought in cardboard, butcher paper, markers, crayons, tape, scissors, staplers, and glue.

He allowed them to pick their own partners. The assignments consisted of the students' building props and writing dialogue to create a public service announcement or commercial. Over the next four days, the students threw crayons, cursed out loud, pushed each other, ran around the room, almost stabbed one another, and made a giant mess. He sat and watched the circus and hoped the principal stayed away from his room. The teacher next door complained about the noise, so Taze allowed him to send his worst students over to his room to join in the fun, which stopped the complaints.

*   *   *

The phone rang hauntingly at 2am. It was Horace.

"Hello," Taze answered.
"When I was 19; I had dreams, aspirations, and beliefs. Now all I have are ten dogs."
"Ten dogs?"

199

"A couple of locals were watching my dog. I gave them money for food and all that stuff, right? And somehow, they got the dog pregnant without knowing and without telling me."

Horace talked more, almost frantic, very loud.

"I had dreams. We both did. Even if we couldn't date, even with all the physical repression we endured, we had dreams!"

*   *   *

"Your moving truck will arrive between 10am-noon on Friday."
"I'll be at work. Can it be delivered after 4pm?"
"Sure. Sometime between 4pm and 7pm on Friday."
"Can you explain how your service works again?"
"We drop off the back of a moving truck. You load it. We come back two days later and take it. You have to be there on the drop-off and the pick-up."

On Friday, Juan rushed Taze home from school. Taze had to get the moving truck parked somewhere along a long stretch of empty parking spaces, but the teens continued to park their cars in these spots. Taze started his wait at 4pm.

"Excuse me. Can you park your car over there? I'm expecting a moving truck. Thank you."

Five o'clock came around quickly and so did six, but no moving truck. Taze paced in the parking lot. Back and forth, over and over. He grew more and more angry and felt more and more like a loser. It seemed like the teens gathered at the window to peek out at him.

Taze simply followed one of the last steps for getting out of West Texas and back to south Florida.

Suddenly, at 6:54pm, he saw a moving truck enter the parking lot.

*   *   *

"Okay class, you can talk to each other, but don't make a mess and keep your hands to yourself."
"Okay, Teacher!"

The students obeyed those instructions for about five minutes when the pushing and yelling began. Taze sat at his desk and thought about the last few days in West Texas. His screensaver clicked on. He downloaded a genuine Earth, Wind, and Fire screensaver several weeks ago. It featured a slide show presentation in chronological order from the band's beginning to the present day.

He transfixed his eyes on the screensaver. One student punched another in the arm, which led to a near riot between opposing groups of eleven-year-olds.

This forced Taze from his screensaver induced stupor. He walked over to the quarrel.

"Okay, break it up."

Spanish words and expressions flew throughout the room. The students still screamed. With little interest, he tried to get them to sit down and be quiet. Another student tossed a miniature nerf football that just missed Taze's head. Suddenly, his computer started playing music. That's when he turned around to see the principal standing behind his desk looking at the screensaver.

The kids didn't even notice that she walked in the classroom. When they did, little voices said, "la directora" repeatedly. The noise from the computer became interpretable when the kids sat down and stopped shouting. It went along with the Earth, Wind, and Fire screensaver. After a couple minutes, the screensaver started to play a midi version of the melody of "That's the Way of the World." The principal appeared stunned.

Taze pitted out, and snots ran down his nose. He wore wrinkled pants and messed up hair. The principal didn't say much, so Taze walked over to her nervously. She walked out. Taz told the students that tomorrow would be his last day even though he knew that he would never return to the school again.

*   *   *

"Horace"

"Yes"

"I'm leaving tomorrow."

"I'm very proud of you. Back to Florida?"

"Yeah, I'm excited but very nervous."

"When are you leaving tomorrow?"

"Four o'clock. Juan is bringing me to the airport."

"Good."

"Thanks"

"I feel it's essential that you listen to Sam the Sham on the way."

"I will. How are you, Horace?"

"I'm dying. The neutropal milk shake ain't what it used to be." Taze heard him vomit as Horace hung up the phone.

*   *   *

"I can't do it anymore," Horace yelled.

"I'm flying to Florida, Horace. I'm leaving in 20 minutes for the airport."

"Prince Myskin, Myskin."

"Yes! Myskin!" Taze replied.

"I love people. I'm too generous. My car got stolen by people I lent $1000. They dumped it at some junkyard. I picked it up and parked it at this guy's house. His wife is yelling at me to remove the car."

"Twenty minutes, Horace, twenty minutes."

Taze stuffed clothes and everything else into a large suitcase. He didn't have enough room for everything, so he used a clear garbage bag as luggage and threw out other stuff.

"Horace," he yelled.
"What?"
"I have to go now. I'll call you when I get to Florida."

*   *   *

"You'll have to take me to Calle Ocho when I visit," said Juan.
"Stay as far away from Calle Ocho as you can. Mexicans aren't welcome." They both laughed. A flicker of energy burst within Taze.

The energy subsided when he entered the airport to see an extraordinarily long line. The line extended into the path of a walkway, so he had to leave space in front of him for people to walk through.

The airport was loaded with military personal dressed in their fatigues ready to go home, back to Kansas or Virginia. The line moved. Taze knew he'd make his flight because he arrived two hours early.

The businessman in front of Taze seemed anxious for conversation.

"Where you headed?" he asked.
"Home. Finally."
"Where's home?"
"Florida. Haven't been there in a year."
"Army, right? Thanks for serving our country," he walked away.

Tazed wondered if he looked like an Army man.

*   *   *

Sam the Sham, John Oates, Peter Fonda. Wooly Bully, Outlaw Blues, *Ulee's Gold*, Earth, Wind, and Fire.

"Sam the Sham is comfort."

".John Oates is comfort."

"Peter Fonda is comfort."

"That's the Way of the World."

Horace- ran out of gas on the Georgia/Florida border- to surprise Taze at the airport.

Taze never slept on a plane but fell asleep and began to dream.

The dream mutated into the twist on stage with Sam the Sham and the Pharaohs, and then in the car on the way to Kingdom Hall. Wooly Bully on Rock, Roll, and Remember. He never understood the words to Wooly Bully, Mango Jerry, and Louie Louie.

He shouted, "Sam the Sham" as he woke up. The light shone inside the window. Forty-five minutes to landing.

*   *   *

Tremendous heat in that tunnel as Taze tasted the leafy fragrance of humidity. The first sane smile suddenly snuck from his mouth as he walked toward the airport light sweating. He moved forward drenched in moisture. He neared the end of the tunnel. An overwhelming breeze of air-conditioned air shook his spine the second he pushed himself out of the tunnel and into the airport. He shivered momentarily. "Did I actually live in West Texas?" he asked.

She immediately hugged him. The woman who waited for him just north of Miami in a newly remodeled condo. She felt healthy. She looked tanned, tall, and wore shorts.

"How did you survive?" Would have been the appropriate question, but instead Taze received the typical question, "How was your flight?"

"Fine . . . wonderful, I'm back . . . I'm back in Florida!"

*   *   *

She decorated the condo perfectly. Old burned-out mirrors and dressers shined again from the sun that exploded through the big windows. Two cats ran around furiously and sniffed Taze. The place smelled like petunias and corn palms.

A giant television mirrored Taze's reflection. He touched the screen slowly with his index finger. "No dust," he thought.

"I have to go to work," she said.

"Okay, see you later." One hour of human companionship with more to come later.

As Taze sat on the new sofa he remembered how her reports occasionally came into West Texas. Painting this room, new rug for that, new shower curtain with royal palm design, new toilet paper roll holder and the cost of all of it, as well.

He saw it now. Every lotion bottle scientifically placed. Every jewelry box positioned perfectly. Bedspread the exact distance from the ground on both sides. Blues that matched. Yellows that contrasted, aqua walls, and granite countertops. His head turned every which way around and around like an indoor cat outside for the first time. Then, he saw a stack of Watchtowers and Awakes. He saw the New World Translation of the Holy Scriptures. He the Knowledge book. The Require brochure. Sing Praises to Jehovah. Time slips. Territory cards.

He got up and grabbed a small piece of paper. On it, a talk assignment. Her talk assignment for that evening. He sat back down on the new sofa and stared at his reflection in the giant tv screen.

*   *   *

In sunglasses, he faced a blue wave very near the eroded shore. African seaweed under his blanket, a breeze that suggested relief from deep fried humidity, a beer in a foam holder that kept the beer colder. Teens surfed. Seniors tanned. A folk singer with an acoustic guitar played to his friends a far too sentimental song considering the surroundings. He sang, "Maybe I could try and catch the wind."

In other directions the spring break crews played without a care in the world. Flossy bikinis, newly inked bicep tattoos, hip-hop, lotion, and volleyball.

All those contemplative beach songs flowed in his head.

Talk back at the ocean.
I want to die in cold water.
I'll be standing on the beach with my guitar.

His buzz sputtered away like an untied helium balloon.

*   *   *

Taze wondered about the man Jesus resurrected from the dead. Since the dead are conscious of nothing, Lazarus probably felt a state of total peace after living an upright and morally acceptable life previous to death. Jesus cried when he found out Lazarus died. They were friends.

The phone rang. Horace.
"Hello"
"Hello"
"Horace"

"Yes."

"How do you think Lazarus felt?"

"Lazarus?" Horace paused and replied, "Oh. Lazarus."

"He must have felt like me."

The Peter Fonda from *Easy Rider* Ending

"I blew it, Horace."

"What? You're living by the beach with a beautiful woman in that condo! You did it. You got out of West Texas. You made it. Now you can have fun. Live the dream!"

"I blew it, Horace."

Part 7- "To walk eternally. In my integrity." (2008)

The filth seeped into his shoes. Taze scrubbed the kitchen floor with the energy of a greenhouse effect polar bear climbing a melting glacier. Water from a hose dripped furiously on one end and flowed slowly like a swollen prostrate urine drizzle on the other. Salted butter, smelly sweat, crab leg juice, and soapy chemicals soaked his feet. The angle of the scrubber measured forty-five degrees from shoulder blade to hip to thumb. The yellowness of its bristles masked the soft shades of seafood kitchen slop with its brushed burned red handle. The water absorbed into his wrinkly feet and created lines that resembled his brain, as if his feet now held thoughts, and his brain now walked. The glow of the yellow bristles hummed into meditative sprinkles, and the swish of the broom cracked through the microwave hiss like a gun shot on a quiet countryside.

Salty Red's Pirate Cuisine: a high priced glorified fast-food chain from Oklahoma to New Hampshire to L.A. to Louisiana, and now the workplace of Taze. He scrubbed the floor and thought of how he got there. His thoughts, deep and hungry, but unable to pinpoint anything specific in them. Nothing came, just a concentrated interpretation of bristles. He could hear the patrons just outside the kitchen door.

"Mama, snow crab. Mama, I want snow crab tonight, for my birthday."
"And my son will get his snow crab tonight!"

More snow crab with ten drawn butters. This Yuma, AZ Salty Red's location stood proudly, surrounded by housing tracks, newly built, and low in cost that attracted all those ex-farmers out of the country and into the suburbs. Every suburb needed a Salty Red's.

The seafood chain that brought hush puppies to Minnesota and salmon to New Mexico and high blood pressure to all.

The owner and founder of Salty Red's, Don "Red" Shrimpton built his dream franchise. As a child, his parents called him salty because of the amount of salt he added to all of his food.

Taze noticed poured the "New Orleans" sauce onto a dinner potion of trout. "Wow, look at the color of that liquid! It appears to have the capacity to impregnate this fish." The asparagus burned the shit out of his hands as he pulled it out of one of the eight microwaves.

The management team included handpicked douches who were filtered over many years through the strainer of corporate submission. The criteria for management:

1. Average to below average intelligence.
2. Willingness to follow all corporate policy.
3. Willingness to put belief in all company propaganda and exercise cognitive dissonance on par with an average cult member.
4. Ability to develop a list of witty remarks aimed to discourage the natural work ethic of a seventeen-year-old.
5. Fifty to seventy hours of work a week on a minimal salary.
6. Dress unimaginatively.
7. Groom like a Mormon missionary.
8. Appear to be sex starved.
9. Understand how to push buttons on a microwave.

Taze fully understood the connection between the mandates of management and the qualifications of elders in The Watchtower corporation.

It was a new location, so Taze started from the beginning. He trained with a new group of people, eager and enthusiastic, ready to tackle the challenge.

Salty loved pirates. Mainly from his lower middle class Pittsburgh roots. Obviously, he loved the baseball team. Salty was crushed the day he found out that Willie Stargell wasn't actually a real pirate. Salty's father slaved for a steel plant and drank heavy in the evening, ignoring his son. So, Salty lived in a fantasy world of buried treasure, deep fried fish sandwiches, and of someday joining the Navy.

Taze's leather shoes cracked like a 1917 catcher's mitt discovered in a Cooperstown attic. They had veins and stiffened up as if heroin were injected for twenty-five years straight. Veins that spurted pus blackness and deviled egg with sprinkled vermillion dots. He could trace the tracks of leather veins as they seemed to attach themselves to veins in his ankles, and he could feel the absorption of fast-food poison running up his legs that seemed to weaken his heart. Cooks tossed the dirty dishes from the main large broiler into a giant white tub where the sizzle sound became addicting. Taze supposed the addiction stemmed from the fact that it resembled the sizzle of bacon cooked over an open fire. So, each time a six-hundred-degree pan was dropped into the tub, memories of early camping adventures sprang from each cook's unconscious. Sometimes skin sizzled when a flaming pan would accidentally brand the Salty Red logo and symbolic ownership into the skin. All the cooks were branded at some point. Long straight burn scars on arms and fingers. Some scars went away with care while others became permanent symbols of the sale of labor power, almost like a tattoo of an ex-lover's name.

The first week of work Taze already brandished three burns from the same source: A six-foot ten guy from Augusta, GA named Devony who always bumped hot bake potato trays into Taze's arms. Devony worked part time at Salty Reds while he played semi-pro basketball for a local team.

Taze said to him one day, "You know, you can go professional, but you have to work on one thing."
"What's that?"
"Your peripheral vision."

The color of over microwaved broccoli started to show up on the edges of Taze's toes.

He never saw so much variety in layers of crust from burnt or dried out food. It was similar to seeing a sunset reflect off the Grand Canyon. Parm crusted Mahi, stuffed flounder, exploded cheese sticks, dried butter like caked urine dribble, each layer stacked upon one another that evolved during slow movement of the average ten-hour shift. Shades of red only imagined in alcohol poisoning vomit or hemorrhoidal diarrhea, shades of brown only pictured in petrified horse shit, all in fast fried food layers. Harsh chemicals were required to dissolve this organism. Chemicals that could penetrate every layer of skin.

Devony carried baked potatoes from the large ovens over to the stainless-steel cooking assembling tables. Everything as hot as a Fred Franz talk from 1974. "Hot Bakes," Devony would speak in a low monotone. Five-hundred-degree pans and since Devony didn't seem to have the capacity to yell, "HOT BAKES!" as a legitimate warning, he always branded people's arms. The first burn hurt and shocked Taze.

During the training period, management took Taze over to a mannequin dressed in the appropriate kitchen clothing. The manager focused his attention on the mannequin's crotch, which led Taze to believe something else might be occurring after hours. Its personality seemed more interesting than that of the manager, and Taze felt that if it could come alive and speak, it would report abuse. Its blank gaze suggested long term abuse, almost as if it resigned to its inhumane reality.

The lobster tank at the front of every Salty Red's displayed the fresh Maine catch. They handcuffed the creatures on the inside who bitterly fought each other for space. Eventually, all would be cut open, and still alive after the incision, the creature would wiggle before it was placed into a steamer. After a few minutes, the shell turned bright red and was placed onto a large oval plate with a side of something salted and buttered, no need for a procession or parade upon death, just a sweaty fat red neck with a full stomach that bounce as he exited the restaurant, winking at the tank as he burped.

Taze's shoes squished, and he asked, "What is trapped in my shoe? Could I drink this bit of water after forty days in the desert? Would it evaporate eventually and return to the sky?"

"Hot steam!" The shout before cooks threw dismembered crab legs into the steamer. The steam burned like everything else in that kitchen. Taze considered his direct view into the microwave as his own personal entertainment. He watched mac and cheese containers explode upon completion. The variety of sauces had initials: BB, TG, LT, HB, LOB, ETC. This made it easier for the non-English speakers to restock. Everyone spoke in code, "Even BB sauce." Anything could have filled those containers. All the "cooks" simply pressed a corresponding button with the initials on the microwave. The instructions:

1. Place the container into the microwave.
2. Look at the chart with the list of buttons to press.

3. If HB sauce says number 1, then press number 1 on the microwave with your finger.
4. Remove the container from the microwave.

Taze watched some of his fellow workers struggle through this process, sometimes placing the container into the microwave, but skipping steps two and three and covering a piece of fish with cold thick sauce. It amazed him that people could get through their worldly lives with limited abilities yet have homes and children and celebrate holidays and birthdays. These people could form sentences and walk erect, and he didn't fault them. He realized that they were all in this together. He realized that life on the outside of The Watchtower carried its large share of daily demoralizing. Each minute in the kitchen consisted of sweat and smell. Each second, a risk at branding an arm or cutting a finger.

Liquid seeped from innumerable sources. Double up on the rubber gloves, so that nothing can penetrate them and get some extra protection against the cast iron heat. If some drops of snow crab juice trickled down the forearm undetected into the small glove opening at the wrist, the fingertip shriveled at a slightly more rapid pace and with a slightly more potent stench.

"Why do my hands smell like my feet? My hands have never smelled like the sweat from my armpits."

Double hand washing after pissing.
Triple hand washing after shitting.

The other cooks consisted of young aimless teens with one foot in the trailer park and undocumented workers who survived on low wages. Taze and the rest of the new workers stood in a row, all of them wore black trousers and white chef coats. They were given two

213

name tags. Roberto in courier font. Lester in courier font. Plain single spaced, no last names, two Jasons, three Juans, and one Del Roy. Hail the Yuma suburbs and to Salty Red who provides them with this opportunity for sustenance. For his graciousness in the midst of financial crisis, his generosity in this forest of agony, his altruism in this time of Nihilism! All the workers stuck in between something. The name tags, uniforms, coworkers, giant ovens, grills, deep fryers, surrounded everyone in his womb.

The top manager, Nathan, stood up to speak. "Welcome all to our family. The Salty Red's family. This is a happy place, a kitchen of dreams, so to speak. The happiest workers in the world at the happiest restaurant in the world. It's not many that get this grandiose opportunity to open a new locale. It's only the few chosen that can build the restaurant from infancy to adolescence to adulthood. Please turn into your menu guidebook, and let's read from page four. Theft is something abominable to Salty Red. He hates it. Theft comes from those who lack the proper fear of Salty Red. He does not tolerate it, and you will be fired immediately upon detection and prosecuted to the fullest extent of Salty Red's law." There was a hush among the workers, a hush of fear. Nathan kept talking, "On a personal note, you may see a lobster tail or a frozen steak and feel like it would take only a second to put in your pocket before the end of your shift and waltz out of here but let me tell you this . . . you are being watched. Do we have cameras set up? No. Do we have alarm systems or tracking devices? No. What we have here is the power of unity. The power of the honesty of each worker. There is a small bonus for those that provide information leading to the detection of a thief. We are watching each other. And remember, if you know of a theft by a coworker and do not report the wrongdoing, you are as guilty as that thief. You don't want to find yourself in the backroom with the three managers."

The workers looked around at each other. This put a wedge into their trust of one another. Nathan concluded, "In order for this kitchen to succeed, we must work together in harmony. You are dismissed!"

Some of the workers gave a strange waving salute as they walked away. Taze wasn't exactly sure what that was all about, but as he walked to his car, he mimicked it and looked up to see one if anyone noticed.

The sand that blew onto the pavement stuck to his shoes in an attempt to grasp to something bigger and more powerful. Each step brought a few more into the realm of the sole. Some would drop off; some would imbed themselves deep and never leave no matter how painfully they were crushed. In an instant a sandbox triangle appeared in the distance and towered over the desert horizon, gleaming in the sunlight, blinding Taze momentarily. He looked down with his menu guide that guarded his eyes. His shoes were missing. They were twenty, maybe thirty steps away.

He looked up, and the manager stood before him.

"Welcome to the team."
"Thank You."
"I understand that you have a lot of experience in the kitchen."
"Well . . . ahhh . . ." He didn't really have much experience. He drafted a fictional resume for the job. On paper, he claimed to be a master line cook with a culinary certificate and loads of beach side experience in Los Angeles. In reality, he hadn't set foot in a corporate kitchen in ten years. Taze continued, "Yes, I worked at a beach pub making shepherd's pie and giblet gravy." The answer seemed to stop the manager for a moment, but he composed himself and responded.

"That's very interesting. It is wonderful to have you on our team."

The conversation ended, which relieved Taze He thought, "I almost said spleen soup."

Taze took a risk a couple years previous and left The Watchtower to explore the grandeur of the worldly life with a worldly partner, Akari. Her parents died in car accident when they drove Akari's old, hip, vintage Volkswagen Beetle during hurricane like weather. She never made it back.

When Taze walked into his studio apartment that evening, his cat appeared angry and disturbed. He ran up to Taze sideways with a puffed tail and a mohawk. He sniffed his shoes and opened his mouth with a tiny noise. The cat looked inside his shoe and found the smushed spiky spine from the end of a shrimp. Taze introduced a new powerful scent into the cat's territory. It couldn't be worried about. Taze had a job now, and his weirdly pleasant parking lot encounter with management proved slightly seductive. Managers, like the elders, carried tiny bits of power, and Taze become conditioned to respond to this power.

The average shift moved like time in a cemetery, but other times it passed like a worm hole in outer space: one second in one place, another second in an alternate universe.

"This is a grill. It must be treated with caution because it is hot. Never touch the surface of the grill while it is hot. It can get up to six hundred degrees and that would cause some damage." He smiled for an immeasurable fraction of a second. "I once saw a cook's mustache get scorched off in a fluid second. And then there was that guy whose fly was down. Lesson? Zipper your pants up, and don't lean over the grill.

That's why we have these yard stick tongs. We have an old saying here at Salty Red's, 'Better to burn your tong than your dong.'" The new cooks walked over to the fryer area. "Here we have three new 'state of the art' deep fryers. These units get the brunt of work during our Popcorn Shrimp Promo month." He asked a question, "Does anyone know what two things don't mix?" Nobody answered. "Oil and water, especially hot water . . . I mean hot oil. This unit will explode if you dump water in it."

They sat us down in the booths and chairs throughout the establishment. Taze sat with two young men. They couldn't have been older than twenty.

"Hi, my name is Taze."
One responded with a handshake, "Doctor, nice to meet you."
"Doctor? Your name is Doctor?"
"Yes." He replied with exasperation, as if he had had this conversation ten thousand times before. "My parents thought that if they named me Doctor, it would somehow unconsciously motivate me to achieve the actual education to be a doctor."

Taze thought to himself, "That's like naming a kid Circuit Overseer."

His explanation continued, "I was born on some commune in New Mexico. It was more like a cult, and the leader was a psychoanalyst."
Taze nodded with understanding. He smiled slightly as if something funny just entered his brain, and he spoke again, "I'm a line cook. Do you think that in a world of six billion, somebody is named 'Line'?"

Taze didn't answer his question, but asked, "What's your last name?"
"Kling."

"I know what you mean Doctor Kling. I was also raised in a cult."

"Really, what's the name of it?"

"I was raised a Jehovah's Witness."

"That's not a real cult. Come to Tres Piedras, New Mexico and see what a real cult is like. The Jehovah Witnesses is like a corporation. I mean in our cult, we had child abuse, shunning, corrupt leaders who we had to have absolute subservience to, and ahh, we had to dress a certain way, and we couldn't have sex. It was awful."

"Unfortunately, that sounds all too familiar to me. I lost all of my friends, and then I was too fucked up in the head to maintain a relationship with the one person who was still my friend and who practically rescued me from The Watchtower. How did you escape?"

"I didn't have to escape. The thing folded because the authorities finally ended it for all the child sex abuse and the cover ups and such."

The other young man stuck out his hand and said, "My name is Texas . . . Texas Watson."

Taze had two new friends.

The manager stood up and announced the start of the employee meeting.

The floors needed scrubbing. All the char from grilled remnants had to be removed with bristles, brooms, brushes, degreasers, chemicals, and toxic cleaners.

Scrub and scrape, love and hate.

Taze started with a sweep of all the small plastic baggies that once housed crab or salmon. He swept the paper coasters and straw wrappers. Nothing could be missed. The managers made sure of it. No scrap of paper could remain. Nothing tucked under a fridge or hidden under a cutting board, everything had to be discarded. Taze filled up three empty tall rubber garbage containers with soapy hot water. He held a bucket and rags. He covered the drains with the rags, so no water could escape until he squeegeed it. He dumped the contents of barrel number one onto the floor. Muscles grew, the handle blood red, stiff as a boner. He scrubbed along the floor, each crevice, the grout the color of mucus. "No, you cannot remove your chef's coat no matter what temperature it gets in this kitchen." The veins in his hands erupted almost through the skin. He started to sweat, and the sweat started to smell. Scraps of fish, bone, butter, and broccoli piled up into a mole hill of waste.

"Look at that concoction of filth," Taze uttered to the closest cook who ignored him. All the other workers were so deeply engrossed in their laborious tasks, that no one cared about Taze's plight. He had to make the garbage invisible before he would become visible again. He thought, "Will my cat recognize me when I return home? Will he think I cheated on him in a moment of weak crustacean passion? Would he understand the scent of the several dead species of sea life? How could I look him in the eye this evening?"

Taze sprayed the mound of debris into an open drain. It clogged. Somewhere down in that pipe the flow of wastewater stopped.

* * *

"Sometimes we have to use caution when serving our guests drinks. We cannot be responsible for somebody leaving this restaurant intoxicated. So, it is incredibly important for us to cut off our patrons, if necessary. Maybe a lonely businessman comes in for a night cap. Is there anything wrong with that? No, of course not. But if he is here to drink away a lost sales deal and then get in his car to potentially kill an innocent kid because of his selfish decision, then there is something

219

wrong with it. We are responsible when others can't be. Aside from preventing drunk drivers from being on the road and the lives we could save, another important reason is the modern-day lawsuit. Yes, servers and bartenders, we can be sued, and Salty Red doesn't deserved to be sued. I have been with this company for twenty-six years consecutively. I was a bus boy, then a cook, a server, a dishwasher, a fry cook . . .you name it, I did it, and now, I am general manager of this establishment. I am loyal to Salty Red and to my two beautiful daughters at home. They are the reason I am here, so if my ass is on the line, guess who pays . . . you do."

The general manager seemed to get angrier as he spoke. Taze had a question that he should have kept to himself.

"Any questions?"
Taze asked, "In light of the recent lawsuit against a popular fast-food restaurant pertaining to the unhealthy fat and salt content of their food, could Salty Red's be held liable for a heart attack or maybe a . . ."

Nathan interjected quickly, and his slicked back hair stood up like a penguin peeing. "No, we are not liable. It is a person's freedom of choice to indulge in whatever food they want as long as they pay for it." At that point, Taze should have stopped. He spoke anyway, "What if the person is obese or if the server discovers that the person is diabetic?"

The general manager walked over to Taze and looked down. His bulky frame of well over six feet appeared twice as large close up. The hair in his nose resembled steel wool fibers with one of them far longer than the rest.

"Young man?"

220

"Yes."

"What's your name?"

"Taze," he replied with the meekness of a newborn fawn.

"Ha, Ha, Taze. Listen Taze, if you want to make it through training week, maybe you should do a little more reading of your menu guide and a little less dissecting of Salty Red's legal liabilities. You got that?"

"Yes. I understand. Read the guide and don't ask damned questions."

Nathan's hands and arms shot into the air with his palms facing the crowd, "DISMISSED!"

That particular moment of the training period stuck in Taze's brain as he looked at the results of the clogging of the unseen underground pipe. Too many of Salty Red's menu items swept and mopped into a tube not designed for such a thick resilient mass.

His shoelaces seemed to regenerate every night as if the chemical and organic combination that penetrated them caused new living cells to grow and prosper. Thoughts of a new life form, a new discovery entertained him as he powdered his feet. "Don't scratch, it will only make it worse. Soak them in salts. Do I need bleach? Could bleach help me escape this darkness? Where is the closest exit?"

*　　　*　　　*

"This is a journey, a journey to the nether regions of culinary arts, an infusion of salt, salted butter, scampi butter, and sea salt, like the infusion of paints in an impressionist painting, a grandiose masterstroke, and a buttery gallop through salty pastures. The horse you ride is a six-hundred-degree oven. This cost Salty Red twelve thousand dollars. That's a lot of pesos! These pie tins serve as a reminder of humility. We have state of the art equipment here, from our dish washing machine to our microwave. Everything is timed and idiot proof. You are the crew, the heart of the house. You will assemble this food, like a puzzle. And when you place the pieces together perfectly, you will have served yourself, the restaurant, and, best of all, Salty Red himself. When Salty left the Naval Academy, he decided to start a revolution. Not a political one, but a culinary one: a food revolt. And his love for the sea and its bounty led him to create aqua farming. Salty does not take from the wild. He harvests all of his seafood . . . I mean our seafood from sections of ocean he owns. His dream became a reality when he mated two distinctly different variety of lobster, and the Salty Red lobster was born. It is a lobster lover's salty wet dream! A succulent shred of meat fattened through lack of exercise and soaked in salt water for its entire life. When a lobster is sent through the oven and the sauce comes out of the microwave, and these two are combined, you have the greatest contribution to the culinary world ever conceived. I humbly present to you the SALTY RED LOBSTER!"

The district manager from corporate held it proudly in the air. It looked different than the standard lobster. It seemed to be missing some parts. Apparently, Salty genetically removed the inedible and less tasteful parts of the lobster. The final result was a giant sea creature that lived its entire life in a small underwater cage alone. It begins its life in a giant salty tank and ends its life in a giant salty toilet.

*   *   *

The busy Saturday night rush began with dates holding hands, drinking wine, and sitting shoulder to shoulder along the tank top people with cheap beer, snow crab, and heavy tan lines on the neck. Their fishing gear sat in the back of the truck, and their mustaches curled in random spots across the lip.

Taze threw two hush puppies into the deep fryer. They floated. The crusty outer shell became a crispy brown color with flakes of residue crumbling off the sides when lifted up in the steel wire basket. The mealy inside of the puppies solidified into a frozen mashed potato consistency. "What mouth would these enter? Who would taste these sodium crumbs?" They served hush puppies with three ounces of popcorn shrimp, six large fried shrimp, and clam strips; all of which were deep fried. There were no timers for the cooking process, only a color chart, a rainbow of browns in which the food had to appear to the naked eye. They discarded anything outside that color spectrum or saved it for the homeless. Sometimes grease splashed up onto Taze's arms and face. He once suggested goggles for protection, but all of the uniforms had to be identical.

The uniforms themselves served as a tribute to pirate fashion. Cooks wore peg legs, eye patches, and a hook on their left hands. Waitresses showed cleavage and dawned large ovular ear and nose rings. Tattoos of ship anchors were encouraged, but not mandatory.

Management spoke, "We have a very special program here at Salty's to help our employees in need. Let's say, you are bitten in the leg by a brown recluse, and the spider bite renders you incapable of working for a short period of time. What Salty does is take twenty percent of your average weekly pay and gives it to you for up to two weeks. That's a very special and generous provision from Salty. Where does the money come from? Well, every paycheck you receive, you can designate the amount of money you would like to donate to the fund. What is this fund called? The doubloon donation. Now, we can't require you to participate, but here are the forms, and it is up to you to help others or not. Each doubloon is worth a dollar. Write the number of the doubloons you want to donate per check." He passed out the forms. All of the employees looked around at each other. "If you plan not to participate, just keep the form." The manager waited silently standing with his arms crossed. Slowly,

Julio wrote a number down and handed it in, then Juan, then Doctor, then Rafael, then Lisa. Taze stared at the form thinking, "My income is $8.50/hr. for incredibly intense labor. If I give up a dollar, that means I'll work one hour a week at $7.50. But if I don't hand this form in, I'll look like some sort of cheap heartless bastard."

Management continued, "Now let me explain employee meals. First of all, no other food is allowed on this property. I don't care if your aunty slaved all night over her famous mustard greens or if abuela Lupe cooked frijoles from scratch, only Salty Red's food is permitted here."

*   *   *

They piped music into the kitchen like sleeping gas at Alcatraz Island. In one month, Taze heard, "Rock Me Gently" by Andy Kim seventy-four times. It seemed obvious to him that the hierarchy of the business felt that up tempo seventies disco was appropriate kitchen music during a lunch rush.

The music continued, "I wanna take you higher!" "I'm takin' what they givin' cause I'm workin' for a livin'." "The heart of rock-n-roll is still beatin' in Cleveland." "Take Me home tonight!" "Theme from Mahogany." "Get down on it."

When Taze arrived home in the evening, his cat ran up to him, took a quick sniff and bolted into his pen. His fur stood up, and he did a very athletic sideways jump. His meow came out as a strange noise that sounded like the word "no." It was a screechy no, a fearful display of angry cat aggression. His sensitivity surprised Taze.

*   *   *

The orders jumped off the screen. Taze pictured waitresses waiting in long ration lines to punch in orders during the big store opening. Doctor sweated like a pro wrestler in a sauna with five Big John Studs. The tall basketball player branded Taze immediately.

Taze thought with anxiety, "Was it something I ate or touched? Is it nerves?" His stomach swirled like a hurricane. He didn't have time for a break, so he squeezed his ass and pulled a muscle in his lower left cheek in the process. A pain ran down his leg like an electrical current through Ben Franklin's dick. He could feel it in his toes, and he almost fell over, losing his balance for a moment. Doctor noticed his misstep and grabbed his arm to support him like a boy scout walks an old lady crossing the street.

"Thanks Doctor."
"No problem. We have a lot of orders man. What's wrong?"
"The D word."
Doctor looked slightly confused, "What's the D word. Disabled?"
"No, not disabled, you idiot . . . diarrhea!"
"Dude, it's too busy for you to shit."
"I got to go man. Imagine trying to plug up Mount St. Helens the second before it erupted."
"What's Mount St. Helen?" he asked.

Taze limped to the bathroom and erupted. He could feel urine rubbing the underside of his thighs because he had no time to wipe off the seat. Water splashed upward like a cool autumn's mist. Taze pictured an abstract expressionist painting.

The managers yelled to Doctor, "Where is Taze?"
"Bathroom, he got sick."

*   *   *

Salty Red survived a similar incident. While a sailor in the Southern California, Salty found a small religious tract on a railroad track. He read the title: "Millions Now Living Will Never Die!" Salty never wanted to die. Actually, he was quite happy. His two favorite books were *The Portrait of a Lady* and, later in life, *Jonathan Livingston Seagull*. He received this tract and thought, "I'd like to be one of those millions who will never die." Suddenly, though, diarrhea struck in a stream of lava that burned his rectum. He darted through the mess hall to the bathroom, but accidentally ran into the officer's bathroom. No toilet tissue at all, not even three and half single ply sheets. Salty remembered the religious tract. He pulled it out of his pocket.

Read or Wipe?

His mind raced as quickly as the habanera juice shot from his asshole.

Read or Wipe?

His fingers trembled a Parkinson's stutter as methane gaily floated freezing his nose hairs.

Read or Wipe?

His toes curled up.

Read or Wipe?

A series of trumpet farts in half second intervals popped like the bubbles exiting a small fish tank filter.

Read or Wipe?

He could feel a layer of film developing like on the top of instant pudding left out overnight. He read the biblical tract instead.

*　　*　　*

A Technicolor snot hung on Doctor's beard guard. The manager ordered Taze to wash dishes for an hour. Water, 165 degrees sometimes 180 degrees, fogged his glasses and shrank his contact lenses. Dishwashing served as the nexus of the wage-slavery restaurant business. The risk of injury advanced because they did not install rubber mats.

Knives thrown into Lake Erie colored water.

He cut his finger on one of the knives and speckles of blood floated at the top of the miniature Lake Erie. Will the addition of platelets and the thousands of red and white blood cells give breed to a new species? He ignored the cut and continued to work. Sweat blackened his undershirt like the missing black top of a street pothole. Crumbles of dissolved deodorant found their way to the thighs of his dark "chef's pants."

A tray got trapped in the conveyer belt that moved the dishes through. This stopped the smooth ride of salad bowls with a clicking sound as annoying and alarming as ten smoke detectors beeping over burnt toast. Taze's reflection in the stainless-steel machine displayed ketchup on his upper cheek (or was it blood?). The click sounded a distinct rhythm: a samba beat from a Casio PT-10 keyboard. He couldn't help but move his hips. As they shifted from side to side the sprinkles of deodorant made their final descent to the soapy foam. Some kind of chemical reaction caused a series of fizzes that mixed with the samba beat like a tribesman dancing for the harvest. He rubbed all the caked deodorant he could in order to fizzle on the two and five beats. He grabbed a plastic ladle and tapped it in sixteenth notes onto the metal edge of the dish table. The knock of the slipped shank of his right shoe and the squish of the deflated air chamber in his left foot had him stomping the back beat.

Left left
right
left left
right
left
right right
right.

Taze, trancelike, recreated some off-Broadway version of Stomp.

On the way to his car, he stepped in pit bull shit. He could see the dog trotting away in the deep desert distance. The color of the mountains matched that of the shit. He noticed corn and squash seeds stuck to the bottom of his shoe. "Was this dog in New England sometime during the 17th century?" He thought, "Should I walk back into the restaurant and get some napkins? Should I attempt to scrape it off with the kind help of the curb or a group of cactus needles? If I do that, some will stuff itself into the traction of my shoe. I'll need a paper clip or tweezers to get it out. Or I could just wait until it wears out naturally."

He chose to do nothing and with an indifferent shrug, got into his car with the freshly laid shit attached to his shoe. The smell intensified in the closed space of the tiny car. Much of the shit transferred to the small, squared sandpaper carpet. He rolled down the window for a moment and realized that the local Yuma dairy farm air smelled just as rancid. Plus, it was about one hundred and fifteen degrees outside. He pondered the subtle difference between the pit bull shit and the cow dairy farm shit. There's always that moment when he enjoys the smell, that split second before the conditioned brain recognizes the scent and identifies it as "bad."

*　　*　　*

Taze entered Salty Red's that morning slightly hyper from two large cups of coffee. When he entered the kitchen, the managers brought him into the bathroom and pointed at the handicap stall. He couldn't help but notice the luxuries that graced the handicap room. Giant sturdy bars like futuristic tunnel transport, a thick foam leather seat about two or three times the thickness of an average seat, soft lights overhead, and a magazine rack with retired persons pamphlets. The manager pointed at the inside of the toilet. It stood laden with fresh heavy stains.

"Did you do that?" Taze paused, and the manager started talking again.
"You're the only cook on this early. It had to be you."

Taze thought of the famous jazz song. He wondered if the songwriter imagined this context when he penned it. Was this scenario his inspiration? He panicked a little, and the smell started to invade his nose holes.

"Did you do that?"
"No sir."
"Fine, but . . . off the record, if this was you who did this, please tell me how."
"What?" Taze asked.
"Listen . . . I've eaten Salty Red's food almost every night for twelve years. I'm all clogged up. I can't take a shit. My long intestine is like the inside of an oak tree."

Mop liquid saturated Taze's shoes. It seeped into his socks and absorbed into his toes. His big toe had developed a black nail. Was it mold? Should he tear off the nail? Will the mold become airborne? Will he inhale it, and will it reproduce in his lungs? Maybe they'll conduct an autopsy and think he smoked cigarettes. Will his lungs liquefy?

Taze exclaimed, "There are no more nows, only a repeat of a previous now. We must digress and return to the first now. What was the now of placing catfish on bun? What did it feel like when you grasped the spiny crab leg and yanked on it without remorse until butter squirted forth and your hand bled? How did it feel? Like a rolling bone? How many exploding volcanoes need to explode in order to return to the first now?"

The texture of soap scum blanketed his fingers and made them smell like the combination of back sweat and crustacean bacteria. The restaurant ran out of rubber gloves, normally a major health issue, but they moved on with the work. Cleaning chemicals absorbed into Taze's skin and eventually his blood stream. It surfed through his veins stopping off at major organs occasionally.

He worked as a line cook and looked in the mirror each morning with post shower snot dripping out of his nose. He worked as a scholar at one point. Maybe not a scholar but a well-educated college teacher. He published things and earned a PhD. So, how did he get here? He remembered when she left and the pictures of them that remained on the walls appeared as real as the Smurfs or the Care Bears. People smiled all around. One with her family and their giant diamonds and upper-class Japanese teeth.